I0582303

# MINT AND MURDER

## A SMALL TOWN CONTEMPORARY COZY MYSTERY

### HEYWOOD HERBALIST COZY MYSTERIES BOOK 3

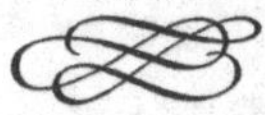

## CARLY WINTER

Edited by
**DIVAS AT WORK EDITING**
Cover By
**COVEREDBYMELINDA.COM**

WESTWARD PUBLISHING / CARLY FALL, LLC

Copyright © 2022 by Carly Winter

All rights reserved.

No part of this book may be reproduced in any form or by any electronic or mechanical means, including information storage and retrieval systems, without written permission from the author, except for the use of brief quotations in a book review.

*This is a work of fiction. Unless otherwise indicated, all the names, characters, businesses, places, events and incidents in this book are either the product of the author's imagination or used in a fictitious manner. Any resemblance to actual persons, living or dead, or actual events is purely coincidental.*

Cover by: CoveredbyMelinda.com

# PREVIOUSLY IN THE HEYWOOD HERBALIST COZY MYSTERIES...

Previously in the Heywood Herbalist Cozy Mysteries...

In *Herbs and Homicide*, daytime soap opera star Samantha Rathbone flees Hollywood, leaving her life literally on fire, and she ends up in Heywood, Arizona. Adjusting to the small-town life isn't easy, but she finds the locals welcoming despite her worries that her true identity will be discovered. She takes a job at Sage Advice, the local apothecary, and tries to settle into a life of anonymity.

When Sam finds her boss, Bonnie, dead, she quickly becomes the main suspect. Surprisingly, Bonnie has left Sage Advice to her and Sam has the most to gain by her death. As Sam struggles to catch the real killer, she also finds herself in a position where she can't trust anyone. Is the killer Bonnie's daughter? Annabelle, Sam's co-worker? Doctor Gerald Butte, the physician who hates Bonnie? Or maybe Doug, the local homeless man who lives under the bridge? He was there that morning…

Meanwhile, in _Lavender and Lies_, Deputy Jordan Branson continues to remind Sam of George Clooney—except when she's mad at him, which is quite frequently. She also discovers her employee and friend, Annabelle, enjoys exacting revenge on those who wrong her and the people she cares about. When their friend, Gina, the dog rescuer / nail salon owner / writer is accused of murdering the most hated man in town, who also happens to be her ex-husband, Sam finds herself once again embroiled in a murder investigation. Heywood is an old town with many secrets, and Sam slowly begins to uncover some of them. This leads to her being able to prove Gina wasn't the killer, yet when the real murderer is revealed, Sam feels terrible about exposing them.

And now on to Mint and Murder…

# MINT AND MURDER

**A dancer is found dead. The killer will go to great lengths to avoid apprehension.**

Deputy Jordan Branson is accused of murder in order to cover up a departmental investigation into his questionable behavior. He asks former Hollywood starlet, Sam Jones, to help him find the real killer.

The problem?

Sam isn't sure she believes in his innocence.

She dives into the case anyway, but unfortunately, all clues lead directly back to Jordan.

Once Jordan's arrested and proclaims his innocence once again, Sam's determined to catch the real killer and continues to prod and question the rest of the suspects.

But will she uncover the truth before the real killer gets to her next?

# CHAPTER 1

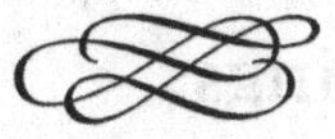

THE LAST THING I expected when I entered the store was to see my employee and friend, Annabelle, doing the moonwalk across the floor with Michael Jackson blaring through the speakers. She'd even donned a silver glittery glove for good measure. Catnip, my feline, and Jack, Annabelle's beagle, stared at her intently, seemingly unsure of what to make of her moves.

I watched for a few seconds, truly impressed. How much time had she put into learning them? I imagined nothing short of a decade or two.

When our gazes met, her cheeks flamed cherry-red and she hurried over to her boom box —a relic from her younger years—and hit the off button.

"Sorry," she said, pushing her already vertical bangs up from her forehead. "I'm getting ready for the dance contest." As she righted her off-the-shoulder neon green sweatshirt, I also noted she'd somehow found matching legwarmers to wear over her brown leggings.

"Dance contest?" I asked absently, weaving through the display table of Sage Advice that had once been covered in flu and cold remedies. Now that spring had arrived, we were focused on allergy tinctures. After I rounded the counter, I stuffed my bag in the cabinet underneath the cash register.

"Oh, my gosh, Sam!" she exclaimed. "Are you kidding me? The Annual Heywood Dance Contest! It's being held at Groove and Go Dance! Haven't you seen the signs around town?"

I tucked a black and gray curl behind my ear. "I'm sorry, but no, I haven't."

Annabelle muttered something I couldn't hear, but I decided to ignore her. Frankly, I'd been too busy to notice any posters about a dance contest. With spring now arrived, I was fully focused on gathering the funds to build a deck out back so we could start serving tea every afternoon. I'd been meeting with a few construction companies in the area and now waited anxiously for their plans and sketches of their visions for the decking. Hopefully, I'd saved enough money to make it a reality.

"The annual Heywood Dance Contest happens the last Friday of March," Annabelle said. "It's almost as big of a tradition as the Christmas Festival."

"Well, considering your moves, I think you'll win," I said, hoping to put an end to the conversation.

"I've won twice," Annabelle said, smiling. "And I want to bring home the trophy again this year."

"You've got this one in the bag," I said, pulling out my phone and checking my email again. Dang it. Still nothing from any of the construction companies.

"Last year, Brittney won," Annabelle continued. "The one who used to work at the sheriff's department. Remember her?"

I nodded, recalling her quite well. A pretty, young girl in her twenties who had wanted to date Jordan, despite him being old enough to be her father. That arrangement always made me cringe, maybe because I'd seen it so many times in my former Hollywood life and rarely did it end well. The young lady usually was trying to climb the Hollywood ladder to fame and fortune, and the older gentleman was simply trying to crawl into her pants, only to discard her once he became bored. I'd seen it dozens of times in my almost three-decade stint in Tinsel Town.

"She did a belly dance which, I have to admit, was really good." Annabelle sighed. "She beat out my moves to Olivia Newton John's, "Physical.""

I vaguely remembered the video—tights, high-cut leotards, sultry glances into the camera. I smirked, trying to imagine Annabelle's version. She definitely had the body to imitate the singer, but did she have the sex appeal? Not sure about that.

"But this year," she continued while slipping off her silver glove, "I'm going to kill them all with a little MJ."

"I think you'll be great," I said.

"Oh! You should totally compete, Sam!" she exclaimed. "You had dance training, right? I mean, you did that one Hallmark movie where there was that dance scene... I can't remember the name of it. It had kind of a Cinderella vibe and you had that waltz scene in a ballroom."

I searched my memory and remembered the film. Not one of my best, and sort of embarrassing. The dance scene she referred to had taken hours upon hours to film, mainly because I'd kept mis-stepping, and at one point near the end of it, I'd accidently stomped on my partner's foot and broke his toe. Both of us had fallen to the floor, my fancy floor-length dress catching on my heel and ripping up the back while he cursed and screamed.

My co-star had been furious with me, as had the crew and director. Even the extras lining the room who had been clapping and acting like they were having a great time had groaned and sworn out loud. I didn't blame them. I'd told my agent, Max Malone, I wasn't a dancer, but he insisted I take the job. It had been a mistake from the beginning.

Sometimes it was hard being friends with Annabelle since she'd followed my career so closely and had the memory of an elephant.

"I think the dance contest will go on just fine without me," I said. "I'm not a very good dancer."

She furrowed her brow. "What about that movie?"

"Editing is an actor's best friend," I said. "Now, let's go over the inventory and figure out what spring-like soap baskets we're going to feature in the online store, and here at Sage Advice."

She sighed and sat down on the stool. "Definitely mint and probably some lemon balm. I was thinking of actually growing mint in some planters outside the front door. It'll be a nice, fresh scent for customers when they walk in. Then, if any of them ask about it, we can point them directly to the mint soap baskets."

"Excellent idea," I said. "I was also thinking we could make a bug repellant since spring is on the way."

"Oh! I like that!" Annabelle squealed. "I'll have to do some research, but that should be easy peasy."

"What do you think about some natural mouthwash as well?" I asked.

She nodded. "It's definitely shaping up to be, like, a Minty March!"

"That's a perfect theme," I replied. "I'll make up some signs and flyers to hand out about the benefits of mint."

We spent the next hour laying out our plans in between helping customers. Every few minutes I'd check my phone to see if I'd received any emails from the contractors. I really wanted to build that deck and prayed I could afford it. But I also was very aware that a watched pot never boils...

"Your deputy has arrived," Annabelle said, elbowing me in the ribs. I glanced up from my phone to see Deputy Jordan Branson swagger into the store giving off all sorts of George Clooney vibes.

"Good afternoon, ladies," he said, grinning.

"What are you doing here?" I asked, refreshing my email once again.

"That's not very nice," Jordan said.

Annabelle nodded. "Right? It borders on rude."

"That it does," he said, grabbing his chest and throwing his head back as if I'd shot him. "What have I done to deserve such treatment from the pretty store owner?"

Annabelle dissolved into a fit of giggles while I rolled my eyes. "Such drama," I said. "You've done nothing. It's the three contractors who haven't gotten back to me who are at the top of my you-know-what list."

"Still nothing?" he asked. "Should I knock down some doors? Make some arrests?"

"That hadn't occurred to me," I replied. "It's a heck of an idea, though."

Jordan winked. "Consider it done." Then he picked up the silver glove from the counter. "Do I even want to know what this is for?"

"It's mine," Annabelle said, swiping it from him. "It's for the dance contest."

"Ah, I see," he replied. "Let me guess… Michael Jackson?"

"Exactly." Annabelle pointed at me. "She won't even enter."

"I don't dance," I muttered.

"You don't dance, you don't date… you are exactly zero fun," Jordan said. Then, reaching over the counter, he took my phone from me, set it down and grabbed my hand.

Before I knew what was happening, he'd pulled me flush to him, wrapped his left arm around my waist, and raised our linked hands. "Personally, I am an excellent dancer," he said.

I was going to argue, but then quickly resigned to the situation. It seemed easier to let Jordan have his way than fight about it.

As he waltzed me through the store humming a tune I didn't recognize, I focused on not stepping on him, staying away from the glass display tables so I didn't knock one over, and trying not to think about how close I was to him.

After a minute or two, he stopped, spun me around in a slow circle, then attempted to dip me.

"Watch my back," I grumbled. "It doesn't bend like it used to."

Chuckling, he pulled me upright. "Funny how that happens after fifty, isn't it?"

I nodded and sighed with relief that I'd successfully maneuvered through the dance I didn't want to perform.

"Wasn't that fun?" Jordan asked as Annabelle clapped.

"Loads," I grimaced. "I need to get back to work."

"Are we still on for coffee in the morning?" he asked.

"Don't you two meet for coffee almost every morning?" Annabelle questioned.

I nodded. "I'll be there at eight."

"Well, I better get back to keeping the peace and serving the great people of Heywood," Jordan said, just as his phone rang.

He pulled it out of his pocket and glanced at the screen, then answered. "Yes, Sheriff," he said. "What can I do for you?"

I rolled my eyes. His boss, Sheriff Mallory Richards, was not my favorite person. I found her condescending, rude, arrogant, and terrible at her job. I'd like to run against her, but I knew nothing about law enforcement.

As he listened intently, his brow furrowed and his face paled. Pursing his lips, he nodded.

Finally, he said, "Right. Okay. Yes. I'll be right in."

After hanging up, he shoved the phone in his pocket. Gone was his light mood. "I've got to go," he said, his voice tight.

"Is everything okay?" I asked, now concerned.

"We'll see." Without another word, he left the building.

"I wonder what that's all about?" Annabelle said.

I shrugged, checking my phone again, an uneasy feeling settling in my chest. "Police stuff. Who knows?"

"You two are so cute together," Annabelle said. I shot her a glare. "But I know you aren't dating," she continued, holding her hands up in front of her.

Just as I was about to set the device down, another email came in. A bid for the deck.

"Oh, my gosh," I whispered, almost afraid to open it. I'd been focused on it for so long, the disappointment of not being able to afford it would be somewhat devastating.

"Look at it," Annabelle said as she peered over my shoulder and nudged my ribs.

I tapped the screen and breezed through the email. I didn't care that Mike from Skyline Contractors had enjoyed meeting me. I just wanted a number.

Once I opened the PDF, I found it.

Annabelle and I traded glances as smiles broke over both our faces.

"We're getting the deck!" she yelled, jumping up and down.

I nodded and threw my arms around her while tears welled in my eyes.

Yes, we were getting the deck.

However, the full elation I thought I'd experience wasn't quite there. Now that I knew I'd be able to afford the decking, I had to get the designs approved by the city. I hoped it didn't take too long.

I untangled myself from my friend and dialed Jordan to share the good news. It went straight to voicemail, which wasn't really odd, but I couldn't shake the feeling something wasn't right.

When he'd left, he'd seemed quite upset, but I'd been so caught up in my own issues, I hadn't realized to what extent, until now.

"Hey, Jordan," I said to the voicemail. "No need to knock down doors and make arrests. I received the bid right after you left, and I can afford the project. Call me when you can."

I smiled as Annabelle prattled on about the

planters she'd seen online that would look super cute lining our new deck and the herbs she wanted to grow in each of them.

Only half-listening, I tried to ignore the feeling of dread building within me.

# CHAPTER 2

Jordan never returned my phone call, which only worried me more. I slept fitfully, getting up often to pace, which annoyed Catnip. Apparently, he was the only one who should be up during the witching hours. As he parkoured my living room then took off out the apartment door into the store, I sat on the couch in the dark with my swirling emotions. Sure, I was thrilled with the coming addition to Sage Advice. But that horrible feeling that something was wrong wouldn't subside. In fact, it only grew stronger.

When the sun peeked over the mountains, I slid into my sneakers and decided on a walk before meeting Jordan. "Bye, Catnip!" I yelled as I hurried down the stairs and out the back door. For a minute, I stopped and stared. I'd have to find a new place for the dumpster, and probably have the walkway to the back redone as I couldn't have customers trouncing through the workroom to get to the deck. It wouldn't be a huge space like the restaurant down the street, On The River, had, but maybe enough for three to five tables and some planters. We'd already worked out that we'd brew the tea in the back room and serve it through the rear door. Every month we'd have different flavors to choose from, along with a variety of pastries.

Yet, I still had doubts I was making the right decision. What if I built the deck and no one came? What if it was nothing but a money vacuum?

I'd go over the numbers again with my lawyer and accountant, Colin Breckshire III. I wanted to make smart decisions, and I wasn't sure this would qualify as one. Was it a vanity project, or good for business? Would five tables offer me enough income to make it worthwhile? Perhaps, but the deck would also bring people in the store. So even if I took a loss on the tea and pastries, I could make up for it in product sales.

Ugh. A risk I wasn't sure I wanted to take, but at the same time, I really wanted that darn deck.

I took the path down to the Riverwalk and inhaled the fresh air. Soon, the river would be packed with tourists taking rafting trips, locals swimming, and all the restaurants and shops would be buzzing.

As I came upon the bridge, I noticed Doug, the local homeless drug addict, sitting on the other side, his head tilted up to the sun.

"Good morning!" I called just as I entered the tunnel. He turned to look at me, bringing his hand up to his face to block the sun.

He smiled broadly as recognition set in. "Sam! Good morning!"

As I emerged on his side, I said, "How is everything going today, Doug?"

"Great! I certainly can't complain."

I'd begun to think of the homeless man under the bridge as some sort of all-knowing-monk type guru. One of the smartest people I'd ever met, I often found myself humbled by his upbeat attitude despite the fact he literally lived under a bridge.

"What are you reading these days?" I asked, glancing around. He visited the library frequently and I often found him with books way above my intelligence.

"I'll go to the library later today, but for now, I'm practicing meditation. It's quite a fascinating experience."

Unfortunately, my meditation experiences had never been positive. My brain was too jumpy and no matter how hard I tried to focus on nothing or my breathing, I quickly realized it was futile. And the thoughts that interrupted my practice weren't anything important, either. Stupid things, like what was the name of the first Jurassic World movie? Why are green beans considered a vegetable while lentils aren't, but they're both under the legume family? When was the last time we got any rain? My mind was like a search engine with too many tabs open.

"I'm glad you're getting something out of it," I said.

"Do you practice?"

I shook my head. "I've tried. Maybe when I do yoga I get to that state a bit, but not while sitting and just being like you are."

He chuckled. "Busy minds lead to chaotic lives."

I smiled and waved, then went on my way. There was still a hint of winter in the air, almost seeming to warn us that it could return at any time. I hoped Mother Nature kept it at bay. I'd hated the snow and cold.

As I continued my walk, I smiled and greeted a few acquaintances. When I reached the end of the Riverwalk, I glanced up to the patch of brown grass where a flock of geese camped out during the summer months and wondered when they'd return. Perhaps when they'd taken up their perch, I'd know for certain spring and summer had arrived.

Climbing the hill that led to Comfort Road, I checked my phone. I would be a few minutes early for my morning coffee appointment with Jordan.

I entered Cup of Go, then stood in line to grab my caramel latte and his black coffee, two sugars, and a dollop of cream. The blueberry muffins looked particularly appetizing, so I grabbed two of those as well. Noticing an empty table by the big picture window overlooking the river and forest, I hurried over and sat down.

The view never became old.

As I sipped my latte and picked at my muffin, I became lost in thought. Maybe decking wasn't the way to go for Sage Advice. Perhaps we could put in a large window in the back room, make that the tearoom, then put the workspace somewhere else. The only way to go was upstairs. Perhaps Bonnie's old apartment could become the place where we made our tinctures, soaps and capsules? But was I ready to clear out Bonnie's things? Probably not, even though I should.

While ruminating, I also lost track of time.

Every now and then, Jordan would run five or ten minutes behind. As I checked my phone, I realized I'd been staring out the window for a half-hour. Glancing around the store for him, I began to worry. Being this late was not like him at all. I sent a quick text and when that went unanswered, I called. That feeling of doom I'd been carrying with me and trying to ignore grew, physically weighing me down.

Finally, he entered the store and made his way through the crowd. I smiled but his brow remained furrowed, his mouth in a fine line. As my stomach clenched, I pushed away the remaining muffin. He sat down across from me, and I noted he wasn't in uniform.

"Jordan, what's wrong?" I asked.

He shook his head and sighed, raking a hand through his thick hair. "I'm… I guess you can say that I'm in trouble."

"What's going on?" I sipped my caramel latte.

"Do you remember Brittney?"

"Sure." The girl who worked at the sheriff's office who had wanted to date him—a man old enough to be her father. Apparently, she was also one heck of a belly dancer, and the winner of the Heywood Dance Contest last year. "What about her?"

Jordan rubbed his face with his palms and I realized he was more stressed than I'd ever seen him. "She's… she's dead," he muttered.

"Oh, no!" I gasped, my hands flying to my mouth. "What happened?"

"It was a murder."

I had no words. Who would want to kill her? No, she hadn't been my favorite person, but she certainly didn't deserve to have her young life taken from her.

We sat in silence for a long moment and I had the distinct feeling there was more to the story. "What else happened, Jordan? What aren't you telling me?"

"Do you remember when Gina was in jail and Brittney was spreading gossip about how she was suicidal?"

"Yes, I do," I replied.

"And then I told you Brittney made some inappropriate remarks to me at work? Did some things she shouldn't have?"

"Of course. She slapped your butt and made some sexual statements to you, all of which you reported. You said her spreading gossip about Gina would be the final nail in her coffin." I winced at the choice of my words which, based on the circumstances, were crude.

He nodded and pursed his lips. "Well, in her exit review, she was told why she was being fired, which also included my statements given about her inappropriate comments and conduct."

"Okay. Go on," I urged. "She's been gone from the department for a couple of months. What does any of that have to do with you now?"

"About a month ago, she filed a complaint with the sheriff's office about me. She... she said I'd sexually assaulted her while she worked there."

My blood ran cold as my heart thundered.

"They opened up an investigation," he continued. "I've been under heavy questioning and this morning, the sheriff officially relieved me from my duties until further notice. It's been stressful as heck because I've never sexually assaulted anyone."

"Jordan, why didn't you tell me all this?" I reached across the table and squeezed his hand.

"We just don't talk about serious things," he

said, shrugging. "I've tried, but you always close up or redirect the conversation."

No lies there, but there was one amendment: I didn't want to talk about anything serious having to do with my own life, but I'd gladly listen to him. However, in the world of relationships, that also meant at some point I'd have to reveal a little of my serious stuff—like my real name and my Hollywood past—which I still wasn't comfortable doing. So, yes, he was right. I was willing to listen, but I wasn't willing to talk.

"Remember yesterday when the sheriff called me while I was in your store?" he asked. "That was more bad news."

I nodded, not sure my heart could take anymore. The fact that he didn't meet my gaze told me what he was about to say would be nothing short of horrible.

He glanced around the shop and leaned forward. "Because of her accusation and the investigation, they also think I killed her... just to make it all go away."

As the words sank in, I wanted to be sick. "They think you killed Brittney to stop the investigation into her claims of you sexually assaulting her?"

He nodded.

I sat back in my chair and studied my friend, having a difficult time believing he could swat a fly, let alone sexually assault someone. "Jordan, I don't know what to say."

"Say you'll help me find the real killer, Sam."

"What are you talking about?" I asked. "You've got to be kidding me."

"No, I'm not. You've solved two murders here in Heywood. Help me do it again!"

Actually, I'd solved three murders, but he didn't know about Gerald, my no-good, fraudulent, money-grubbing dead husband.

"Brittney was a dance instructor at Groove and Go Dance Studio," Jordan continued. "She took a job there after she left the sheriff's department. It had to be someone there, or the boyfriend... we need to find out who killed her."

"Why does the sheriff think it's you?" I asked. "Why isn't she investigating anybody else?"

"Because I'm an easy target," Jordan said. "I basically got Brittney fired, then she brought those charges against me. In order for them to go away, I killed her. It's neat and tidy for the sheriff and she won't have to do much work."

"She'd seriously let you go down like that?" I asked.

"In a heartbeat," he replied.

"Why, Jordan? Why wouldn't she believe her deputy?"

He sighed and closed his eyes. "Because of my time as a cop in Chicago," he said. "Because of what happened there."

# CHAPTER 3

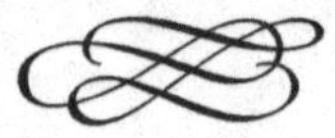

I COULD SEE the pain in his gaze as he stared at me and I knew we were headed down a rabbit hole of serious, life-changing conversation. Exactly what I didn't want.

But he also waited, as if hoping I'd give him permission to keep talking, to reveal his secrets and sordid past. Well, I had to assume it was sordid. It had led Sheriff Mallory Richards to believe he murdered Brittney.

As I squirmed in my chair, I continued my internal debate. Did I want to go down this road of honesty and openness? Or was I ready to pivot and talk about the weather?

Jordan's gaze wouldn't allow for the change of conversation to the mundane. I cared for him, but

I wasn't sure I wanted to dive into his past. Something told me our relationship would never be the same. Yet, I couldn't get up and walk away.

"What happened?" I asked, reaching for my coffee with a shaky hand.

He sat back in his chair and sighed, as if relieved to finally get his story off his chest. "When I lived in Chicago, I was married," he began.

The ill feeling I'd had since the prior day continued to grow, and I couldn't place why quite yet. So what if he was married? He'd been in Heywood for years, so this occurred long ago. Then why did I feel so sick?

"After ten years of marriage, my wife decided she and our daughter would be better off without me, so she asked for a divorce," he said.

Okay, nothing wrong with that. The night before Gerald had been killed, we'd decided to divorce. So far, the story didn't seem so awful, except my empathy for the child. Growing up without a father had been difficult, especially since my mother had been a drunk. I recalled many, many nights where I'd pray for my dad to come rescue me from her, even though I'd never met him.

"Why did she think she'd be better off without you?" I asked.

"The long hours. Some dramatic mood swings. The violence I was exposed to grated on my soul and gave me insomnia." He shrugged. "Usual cop stuff."

I'd never seen any evidence of these mood swings and I found Jordan to be good natured most of the time. But certainly, policing in Chicago was quite different from policing in Heywood. Cows didn't carry guns, the town shut down early, and my understanding was most of the drunks around the area were amiable, not violent.

"Go on," I said. "What happened after she asked you for a divorce?"

"I moved out," he replied. "And tried to figure out how I was going to survive with alimony and child support payments. Don't get me wrong, I loved my little girl and I'd have done anything in the world for her but carrying two houses on a cop's salary isn't easy."

"Didn't your wife work?" I asked.

He nodded. "Part-time. We didn't want our daughter to be a latchkey kid. My wife asked me to help her keep the same hours. Both of us felt it was important for her to be there for our daughter."

"What's her name? Your child?"

"Mattie," he said a wistful smile tugging at his lips. "My little Mattie."

"So, what happened?" I asked. "Why would a divorce lead our sheriff to believe you'd kill Brittney?"

"It wasn't just the divorce," he said. "I found out that my ex-wife, Victoria, began openly dating before the ink was even dry on the divorce settlement. Then I discovered she'd been having an affair while we were married."

"With the same guy?" I asked.

"Yes. And that guy also happened to be a homicide detective in my station," he said. "It was bad enough that she'd left me for a cop, but the worst part was that she left me for one of the most dishonest, reckless men in the department. He'd been investigated many times for use of unnecessary force and stealing, but the department seemingly didn't want to make the charges stick. The guy was slicker than Teflon. He also had one of the highest case clearance rates, and those numbers are very important to the brass and the people who run the city. Paul Newsom was his name."

"I'm sorry to hear that, Jordan," I said.

"So was I." He crossed his arms over his chest. "That divorce just about sent me over the edge. I felt like my life was over. I loved my family but also wanted the best for my ex, so I tried to let her go. I spoke with Paul one afternoon in the parking lot at work and told him he better be good to Victoria and Mattie."

"That seems like a reasonable thing to say," I offered. "You wanted your family taken care of."

He nodded and pursed his lips together. "Well, it was about two months after the divorce, and I had Mattie for the weekend. She told me she'd seen Paul smack Victoria around when they were arguing."

"Did you confront him?" I asked.

"Well, first I wanted to make sure it was true. Mattie was eight at the time, and I knew the divorce was hard on her, so I had a long talk with Victoria," he replied. "She denied it, but I also noticed she was wearing a little more makeup than usual. Maybe to hide some marks he left? I couldn't be sure, but decided I needed to keep watch over her and Mattie."

"What does that mean?" I asked. "Keeping watch over them?"

"It means I lived in my car for the next week, parked down the street from their house. I became completely obsessed with Paul's comings and goings. When he was there, I snuck around the outside of the house trying to catch him beating on Victoria, and God help him if he laid a hand on my daughter."

"And did you?"

He shook his head. "I talked about it more with Mattie, and she said she missed me and didn't like Paul. So, was she trying to get me back in the house? Or had she really witnessed the abuse? I'll never know."

"Why's that?" I asked. "Can't you talk to her now and question her? I mean, she's older and can shed some light onto her thought processes if she can remember them. How old is she?"

"She's dead," Jordan said. As the breath left my body, he continued, "And so is Victoria."

As I stared at him, my mouth agape, I shamed myself. I should've known. Never had he brought up his daughter before, and even if I kept our relationship somewhat frivolous, he would've mentioned her.

I didn't know how long had passed before I could breathe again. "I'm so sorry," I finally whispered, the Band-Aid of my own loss now ripped off and my wound reopened. My pain ripped at my heart, bringing to the forefront my hatred for what Gerald had done to my life and overwhelming sadness for the man sitting across from me. "What happened, Jordan?"

After taking a long drink of his now-cold coffee, he continued. "I heard rumblings around the station that Paul and Victoria weren't getting along. Finally, logic took over and I realized I wasn't going to be able save Victoria if she didn't want saving, so I decided to mind my own business."

We sat in silence for a few moments and I realized he was coming to the pinnacle of his story. Fear squeezed my chest as my stomach flipped, my dread now ten-fold from when he'd first sat down.

"A week later, they were dead," he whispered. "They went peacefully in their sleep. A gas leak in the house was ruled the culprit. They never knew what hit them."

The pain radiated off him as tears welled in his eyes. After a moment he shook his head, as if to clear his thoughts. "But obviously, it didn't end there. Paul said it was a homicide and I was responsible."

Well, sucker punch me in the gut. I never saw that one coming. "How did he make that leap?" I asked.

He stared at the table for a long while before

answering. "Well, with Paul's encouragement, Victoria had installed cameras around the outside of the house. I was so focused on catching him manhandling Victoria, I never even noticed them when I was sneaking around the house. Paul said I was responsible for their deaths, and he had video proof. He brought out the footage of me creeping around at all hours of the day and night."

"What was your motive?"

"That I wasn't happy with Victoria for hooking up with Paul. That I killed them because I was out of my mind with grief over the divorce and me losing my family to him. If I couldn't have Victoria and Mattie, then no one would."

"And your supervisors believed him," I concluded.

"Yes," he sighed. "I fully admit, I looked deranged in the video footage—completely out of my mind. And I suppose I was, but I'd never hurt my girls."

"So, what was Paul's theory? How did you do it?" I asked.

"The night it happened, there was a storm with really strong winds. The power went out, so the cameras weren't working. According to Paul, I used the storm as cover to break into the house and loosen the gas line. Then, I left my baby girl to die."

"I'm so sorry, Jordan," I said. "I can't imagine you doing such a thing."

He smiled, his gaze still filled with a level of sadness most people would never understand. "But the story doesn't end there."

"Oh, my word," I muttered. "Why do I have the feeling this only gets worse?"

"Because it does." He took a deep breath. "Paul was determined to see me rot in prison for the death of my family. For him, there was no other explanation, and he pushed and pushed the department until they opened a full investigation on me. I was put on paid leave, which, in retrospect, was probably a good thing because I could barely function. Paul claimed he saw me at the house the night the girls died, sneaking around. Apparently, we had quite the confrontation, and he chased me away until he caught a case and had to leave before the power went out. When the storm hit and the power did go out, that's when I snuck in and killed my family."

"But you never had that confrontation?" I asked.

Jordan shook his head. "Nope. Never happened. I was at my apartment, alone, and unable to prove it."

"Well, obviously, nothing came of his witch hunt," I said. "You wouldn't be here telling me this story."

"Nothing came of it because Paul died," Jordan said. "He was shot in an alley one night, point blank. They lost their witness and the investigation went away."

It took me a moment to connect the dots. "Did they think you shot him?"

He nodded. "They did. Without Paul there wasn't any case against me, which was quite convenient for me."

"Who do you think killed Paul?"

"I have no idea. My guess is he got himself into some illegal drug scheme. Maybe he had one of the gangs pay him off for him to turn the other way on their illegal activities, then he decided to get cocky and raise his prices. They got rid of him. Something like that. There were always rumors of him being involved in illegal actions, but no one had ever looked into it. He covered his tracks well."

"Once Paul was gone, what happened?"

"After that, I left Chicago, hoping to live out

the rest of my years in a quiet, peaceful place, without a lot of drama."

It was the same thing I wanted, and I found it odd we'd both ended up in the same town. "How did you pick Heywood?"

"I pulled out a good, old-fashioned map, shut my eyes and stabbed it with a pencil. Heywood it was."

We stared at each other for long moment, then I said, "So the case against you killing Brittney is very similar to what happened to Paul."

He nodded.

"In both circumstances, the one person who could send you to prison is dead."

"And I had nothing to do with either," he stated so firmly, I almost believed him.

Almost.

# CHAPTER 4

My phone buzzed just as Jordan said, "So, what do you think, Sam? Will you help me find out who killed Brittney?"

Glancing at my device, I saw Annabelle had texted me. I picked it up. *Mayday! Mayday!* She'd typed. *Butte is here!*

Doctor Garrett Butte was the local practitioner who had been at odds with my old boss, Bonnie, before she died, and now stopped in to give me the riot act every now and then. He called herbalism witchcraft and believed that everyone should treat every malady with a prescription. He also wanted Sage Advice to be boarded up. I referred to him as a licensed drug dealer and sweet Annabelle was afraid of the old coot.

With a groan, I stood and met my friend's gaze. "I'm sorry, Jordan. I have to go. Butte's harassing Annabelle."

His face fell, and I realized he thought I wasn't going to help him. "I appreciate everything you've shared with me," I said. "And I'll do what I can to help you."

"Can I call you later?" he asked.

"Of course." I grabbed my bag and hurried out the coffee shop, hating that I lied to him. I wasn't sure if I wanted to help him find the killer or not. His story had shaken me to my core.

Sage Advice was only a few short blocks from Cup of Go, and my thoughts scattered as I walked. Mentally preparing for Butte while trying to digest everything Jordan had shared caused a horrible headache to form behind my eyes. I couldn't do both, so I concentrated on doing battle with Butte.

Before coming into view of the store, I stopped, closed my eyes, and took two deep breaths. I had to bottle up my emotions from my talk with Jordan and bring my character, Cassie, from *As The Years Turn* front and center. She could handle anything, even an old doctor who hated me, my store, and every plant within it. Cold, calculated and ruthless, she was the perfect match for Garrett Butte.

I marched up to my store and heard Butte yelling something about garbage before I could see him. As I flung open the front door, both Annabelle and he turned in my direction. Before he got a chance to speak, I narrowed my gaze and pointed at him. "What do you want?" I asked, my voice quiet and deadly.

He lifted his chin defiantly and threw back his shoulders in a show of toughness, but I could see the fear in his beady eyes and frankly, I liked it. It only fueled my performance, like adding gas to a fire. "You stole another one of my patients," he replied. "And don't you point at me."

I quickly walked toward him, careful not to bump into any of the glass display tables, and stood before him. Then, just because he didn't want me to, I pointed at him again, my finger waving just inches from his face. "We don't steal anything, Doctor Butte. We help people who come in here looking for relief. Do I need to go over our protocols with you again? Has your aged brain forgot about them so quickly? Guess what? We have an herbal remedy for that."

Okay, low blow, even for Cassie. But I was

emotionally drained from my chat with Jordan and the wild story he'd shared, and I was so, so tired of this petty man in front of me trying to shut my doors. In his seventies, I had no doubt he was sharper than any knife in a chef's kitchen. Memory issues were still a way off for him, but I just wanted him gone, and if insulting him got me the desired outcome, I had a few more zingers in my back pocket. Male impotence, anyone?

His nostrils flared as Annabelle gasped. "How dare you," he hissed.

"How dare *you*," I said, throwing my hands up. "In fact, let's play a game. I dare you to get the heck out of my store and never come back. Leave us alone, Garrett Butte. Go back to pushing your pills on those who will take them. We can both survive in the same area because our customers, thankfully, are *not* alike."

It was the truth, to a certain extent. Our clients preferred natural remedies, but we also welcomed those who were big believers in pharmaceuticals when the pills weren't effective for them or gave them horrible side effects.

"Your plants are going to hurt someone!" he yelled. "This place of witchcraft should've been shut down years ago!"

"What are you going to do?" I chided. "Burn it to the ground?"

"Don't give me any ideas!" he screamed.

"I'm going to get a restraining order against you!" I shouted. "I never want to see your cranky face in here again!"

I'd threatened this once or twice before, but I'd never followed through with it because of the paperwork required. Jordan told me I really didn't have cause, but this time I had a threat. Or what I took as a threat, anyway. I also had my contact at the sheriff's department off duty and under scrutiny for killing a young woman. Sheriff Mallory hated me just enough to tell me I had no case.

Jordan had picked a bad time to murder Brittney, or at least get caught up in the investigation of her death.

Dang it.

"You haven't heard the last of me," Butte growled as he stomped toward the entrance.

"That sounds like a bad movie from the seventies," Annabelle muttered as the door closed behind him.

"Agreed," I said, then turned to her. "I hope he didn't give you too much grief. You shouldn't have to put up with that."

"No one should," she stated. "He makes me, like, so dang mad. He came in here and told me my tinctures were garbage. Do you know how hard I work on those to make sure they're perfect?" Tears welled in her eyes and my anger flared again. The gall of the man.

"Annabelle, everyone knows your work is superb. Don't let that jerk get the best of you, okay?" I gathered her into a hug as she sniffed. "Don't let him do this to you. You're a healer, Annabelle, and the best one in the area, if not the western United States. Don't let him destroy your confidence."

She nodded, then pulled away and swiped at her cheeks. "Thanks, Cassie. I mean, Sam."

I smiled, but realized I was on the verge of tears as well. I needed a few minutes to myself. "I'm going to run upstairs for a bit," I said, "but I'll be right back, okay?"

"Sure," she chirped. "Take your time." And just like that, my upbeat Annabelle was back.

I hurried up the stairs and opened the door to my apartment. Catnip greeted me by running in between my legs, almost causing me to fall. I swore sometimes it was intentional. As I sat on the couch and leaned my head back against the cushions, exhaustion overcame me, and it wasn't even ten in the morning.

Jordan. Darn it. What was I going to do about him?

My instincts told me to get the heck away from his situation as fast as I could. Or was it my trust issues whispering that? Sometimes, it was hard to tell. He never should've asked for help from me, a woman who had a hard time putting her faith in anyone. I guess it came down to whether I believed his story or not. And even if I could convince myself that I did, I'd still second-guess and doubt my judgment.

"Thanks, Gerald," I whispered. "This is all your doing, you jerk."

Dang dead husband.

What were the chances that a cop could be accused of killing someone twice in order to cover up an investigation into him? Statistically, I imagined they were quite low. That right there should've been my red flag.

But it was Jordan.

I'd always found him to be an honest and decent man, and even though he'd angered me many times, it was usually because he was simply doing his job. I believed his intentions were always good and he wanted to help others, which was why he became a cop.

And besides, I'd seen the pain in his gaze when he spoke about Mattie. Never having kids, I couldn't imagine the anguish losing a child could bring. When I heard about people who kill their own children for one reason or another, I always believed mental illness was a factor, something I just didn't see in Jordan.

But what if I was wrong? What if he was an evil, horrible man who had done all the crimes he'd been accused of, and was now looking to slither out of another one?

He could've just gotten in his truck and left Heywood, never to be seen again. Certainly, he'd know how to live under the radar. Heck, he could've made a run for the border. Mexico was only a few hours away. Instead, he'd stuck around and asked me to help clear his name. And he'd confided in me things that brought him obvious pain. The conversation hadn't been easy for him.

Was I looking for an upstanding man that wasn't there?

During my Hollywood nightmare, I hadn't believed for a second that Gerald could've embezzled millions of dollars from our friends and acquaintances, but he had. When I finally accepted the truth, I'd been furious and emotionally destroyed. I'd placed my faith in him and he'd stomped all over it. I couldn't live through that with Jordan. I didn't want to be that sucker again.

But there was something different about Jordan. He held different personality traits than Gerald. Looking back on my dead husband's crimes, I realized I should have seen the signs—the stress, the secrecy, him pulling away from me. And maybe, on some level, I had subconsciously recognized them because I'd asked for a divorce the night before he was killed.

None of those warning bells emerged when I thought of Jordan. Or, were they there and I didn't want to acknowledge them?

With a groan, I stood and began pacing my small living room. Yes, I'd said I'd help Jordan, but that didn't mean I had to. I could easily explain that I wasn't comfortable being in the middle of such an explosive investigation. He allegedly murdered the woman who had accused him of sexual assault—and the case oddly mirrored the one he'd found himself embroiled in years before.

But it was Jordan.

As my phone rang, I fished it out of my

pocket. The man himself. I let the call go to voicemail.

It rang again a few moments later. Jordan again. Cursing under my breath, I picked it up. "Hey," I said. "I was just thinking about you."

"I'm sure you were," he replied. "I was wrong to ask you to help me. If we could just forget about that whole conversation and go back to being friends and talking about mundane stuff, that would be perfect."

Yes, it would, except I didn't think I could do that. "Why do you say that, Jordan?" I asked.

"I just put you in a really difficult situation and I'm sorry, Sam. I shouldn't have dragged you into this."

He had just presented me with the opt-out button. I could walk away from him and his troubles and go on living my quiet, unassuming life.

Except I couldn't. If I dove into trying to solve Brittney's death, I could prove to myself that I wasn't wrong about Jordan, that he was the honorable and honest man I'd grown to know.

And if he was guilty, I could send his pathetic butt to jail, to make him pay for his crimes against not only Brittney, but his family. The case had just become my own litmus test. Was I a good judge of character, or not?

"Sorry, Jordan," I said. "You don't get to brush me off that easily."

A long pause sat between us. "What does that mean?" he finally asked.

"That means I'm going to find out who killed Brittney," I said.

# CHAPTER 5

I DIDN'T TELL Annabelle my plan, nor had I shared it with Jordan. Instead, I asked her to accompany me on an errand, and I told Jordan I'd be in touch with him soon. I needed to put some distance between me and the deputy. If he didn't know what I was up to, he couldn't contaminate or sway my personal investigation. In fact, if he stayed home for a week or two eating bonbons and watched daytime television, I'd be happy. Unless he came across reruns of *As The Years Turn*. Then we may be having a completely different conversation where he accused me of lying about my true identity. I preferred him to answer my questions regarding his truthfulness than the other way around.

"Where are we going?" Annabelle asked as she started up her car.

"Groove and Go Dance Studio," I replied. I figured if Brittney had worked there, it was a good place to start poking around into something that was absolutely none of my business.

"Oh, that's perfect," she said. "If they set it up as they have in the past, I can do a quick walk-through."

"What does that mean?" I asked.

"That's where the dance contest is, Sam! If I can get a better feel for the space, I'll really be able to nail my routine and beat the pants off Brittney."

I'd forgotten Annabelle didn't know Brittney had died. "You won't have to worry about her," I said. "She was murdered."

Annabelle gasped and swerved her car, almost plowing into oncoming traffic. I grabbed her and the steering wheel, which overcorrected us and sent us into the parking lot of a small hotel.

"What the heck?!" Annabelle yelled, finally pulling over. "Don't ever grab the steering wheel like that, Sam! And what do you mean, she was murdered? Do you think maybe you could've delivered that news a little more gently?" We stared at each other a long moment then she shouted, "What is wrong with you?!"

I honestly didn't know where to start then figured, the truth might be a good place.

With a long sigh, I gathered my thoughts. "Brittney was killed and Sheriff Mallory thinks Jordan had something to do with it."

"Why is that?" she asked.

I didn't feel comfortable revealing Jordan's painful past, but I did have to level with Annabelle, at least a little. "Brittney brought up charges of sexual allegations against Jordan. Mallory thinks he offed her to kill the investigation."

"Well, we know he didn't do that," she said. When I didn't answer she reiterated, "Right, Sam? He didn't murder Brittney."

"Of course not," I replied, hanging on to a few shreds of hope that Annabelle was correct. All the evidence pointed to a different answer.

"So what's the plan?" Annabelle asked. "Why are we heading to Groove and Go?"

"Because that's where Brittney worked. I figured it was as good of a place as any to start looking for the real killer."

Annabelle stared out the windshield and nodded. "Yes. That's a great plan. What's our story?"

"I don't know what you mean," I replied. "What story?"

With a long sigh, she rolled her eyes. "You of all people should know this. We can't walk in there and start asking questions. We need a cover story. Why are we there? What's our plotline, Sam?"

Honestly, I hadn't given that any thought, but she had a valid point. Some actress I was.

"I know!" she yelled, bouncing in her seat. "We're going to take dance lessons!"

"No," I said. "Absolutely not."

Her smile faded and she turned to me. "May I be honest with you?"

"Of course," I replied.

"Based on your performance at the store, you're a terrible dancer. Dance lessons would be good for you."

I groaned and shook my head. "If *you* want to take them, then please do so."

"So your grand master plan was to walk in and start asking a bunch of questions?" she asked.

"Yes. I've done it before, so I don't know why it would be a problem now."

"Because this is a dance studio," Annabelle said. "People are there for one reason—to dance.

It's not like marching into a bar or restaurant and striking up conversations."

Well, she may have a point. "I don't want to take dance lessons," I whined.

"They'd do you some good," Annabelle said. "Who knows when you'll be invited to some event where you'll need to dance?"

"Well, so far, that hasn't happened," I sulked. "You sign up for them."

"It's not a good idea," she said. "I'm really too good for lessons. I'm a fabulous dancer."

With Annabelle usually being somewhat humble, I found this brag surprising.

"I bet Gina needs dance lessons," she said. "She's as clumsy as they come."

"That's because she's always got dogs under her feet," I replied. "I've never seen her dance, though."

Annabelle pulled out her phone and dialed. After a moment, she said, "Hey Gina. It's Annabelle."

They exchanged pleasantries, then Annabelle said, "I need you to come down to Groove and Go Dance." Then she put Gina on speakerphone.

"Why do I need to go down there?" Gina asked.

"Because you need to take dance lessons with Sam."

I almost argued, but then decided it wasn't a half-bad idea. Spending time with Gina was always fun, and no doubt she'd make dance class ten times more interesting.

A moment of silence ensued, then a litany of curses. "Under no circumstances will I be taking any dance lessons," Gina muttered. "I've got better things to do with my time. And why the heck is Sam doing that?"

"Because she's trying to catch a murderer," Annabelle said.

Gina groaned. "Not this again."

"Yes, this again," I said. "And to kindly remind you, I did get you out of jail. I think you owe me."

"Low blow," Gina said. "Anything but dance classes, Sam."

"Come on," I said. "How bad can it be?"

After a long sigh, she said, "I'm on my way down. But if I do this for you, we're even. Got it?"

"Yes," I said, smiling at Annabelle. "I'll never bring up the fact that I saved you from going to prison for killing your ex-husband again."

"You're a jerk," Gina said, then hung up as Annabelle and I laughed.

While we waited for Gina, Annabelle said,

"I'm surprised you didn't have dancing classes. You always looked so graceful on the red carpet."

Ah, yes. The red carpet. A carefully scripted show when I was told where to stand, what cameras to smile at, how long to stay in one spot, and then led to the next. It wasn't hard to mess up the red carpet.

I'd worked for months with designers to decide on a dress, as well as shoes and jewelry. A week beforehand, I'd wear the shoes wherever I could to learn to be comfortable in them. Sometimes at work, a lot at home. My practice didn't always prove to be beneficial, though. Remember when actress Jennifer Lawrence fell while climbing the stairs at the Grammy's? She wasn't the first. Thankfully, my tumble at the Emmy's hadn't been televised because it had been a lot worse than hers. She fell gracefully on the steps. I tumbled backward, the skirt of my dress flying up into my face, giving the people on stage a glimpse of my thong. There are no words to describe the mortification and humiliation I suffered for months after as my castmates called me Red, the color of my underwear I'd put on display.

When I'd watched Jennifer Lawrence take her tumble, I most certainly felt sorry for her. At the same time, my own humiliation resurfaced. She had no idea how bad it could've been.

"I remember that one year you were nominated for an Emmy," Annabelle continued. "You wore this beautiful navy blue and rhinestone dress. Your hair floated around your shoulders like black silk. You smiled like you were aware you resembled a goddess."

Huh. I didn't recall such a dress, but after a couple decades, that was to be expected. Either that, or my menopausal brain had erased the memory. "I didn't win, did I?"

She shook her head. "No. Someone else did, but you definitely were the best dressed."

It intrigued me that Annabelle remembered so much of my life in Hollywood. She'd been a true fan of the show, and the fact I'd ended up with my own personal historian as a friend was both interesting and, sometimes, appalling. She recalled things I didn't, which made me question my mental capacities and my Hollywood life in general. It all seemed so frivolous, so utterly ridiculous now, and maybe it had been because I certainly didn't remember the things Annabelle did.

"Here comes Gina," she said, pointing at the car pulling into the driveway.

While Gina parked a couple spots away from us, we exited our vehicle. As we approached her, I smiled, but she pushed her tortoise framed glasses up her nose, crossed her arms over her chest, and glared.

"This is bribery, you know," she said.

"I think it's actually extortion," Annabelle replied.

"Either way, thanks for coming," I said, taking her into an embrace. "I appreciate it."

"You're lucky I like you," she said. "Because I wouldn't do this for anyone else."

Guilt washed through me as I fought to smile. I still hadn't told Gina who I really was, or about my lying, cheating, no-good embezzler husband. The more time that passed, the harder it became. Sometimes I wondered if it really mattered, but in a relationship there was usually some mutual trust and respect. Me not sharing my past with her made me feel ungracious to our friendship, especially since Gina had been an open book and told me all about her life.

"So what's the deal?" she asked. "Why are you putting me through this miserable experience?"

I gave her the quick rundown of Jordan being accused of murdering Brittney and how I told him I'd help find the killer. "It's not like he can go in there and start playing cop," I finished. "He's one of the suspects."

"And you don't think he had anything to do with it?" she asked.

"No, I don't," I replied.

"What do I need to do?" Gina sighed. "Just play along in class?"

"That's it," I said.

"For the record, I'm not doing any recitals," Gina said. "That's a hard rule that won't be broken."

"It's fine," I said, certain I wouldn't take part in any recital, either. "We'll make it fun."

"While trying to find a killer," Gina muttered, shaking her head. "Murder and fun don't belong in the same sentence, Sam. This could be dangerous."

I glanced at the building and grimaced. We had no proof that anyone inside had anything to do with Brittney's murder.

But, if they did, how dangerous could a bunch of dancers be?

# CHAPTER 6

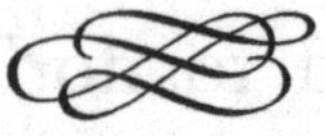

Upon entering, we stood in a huge studio lined with mirrors and ballet bars. The light wood floors gleamed under the fluorescent glare from above. At each end of the room stood an arched doorway. Annabelle slipped off her shoes and immediately began walking the length of the space, mumbling to herself, leaving Gina and me at the entrance.

"Are we supposed to take off our shoes?" Gina whispered. "I hope not. My socks don't match."

"I don't know," I replied as a woman emerged from the arched doorway to our left. "But I think we're about to find out."

"Please remove your shoes if you're coming in any further," she called as she approached, each step a graceful dance in itself. She wore pink ballet shoes, a white leotard with matching tights, and a black dance skirt swirling around her thin thighs.

"What can I do for you?" she asked, smiling. Little lines appeared around her eyes and her blonde hair was pulled in a bun so tightly, it dislocated her eyebrows upward. I pegged her to be in her forties.

"We were interested in some dance lessons," I said. Out of the corner of my eye, I noted Annabelle moonwalking.

"What kind were you interested in?" the woman asked.

I shrugged, unsure what to say. I wanted exposure to everyone in the studio and I wasn't sure what class would provide that. "We're looking to take up dancing for exercise and fun," I said. "What do you recommend?"

"Do you have any prior dance experience?" she asked. Gina and I shook our heads. "Then I would recommend our thirty-day dance package. You can experience all our classes—ballet, waltz, tap and Zumba—and decide what you prefer."

"Are you the owner?" Gina asked.

"Yes, I am," she said, bowing her head slightly. "My name's Katrina Warner."

"I'm Gina and this is Sam," Gina said, hitching her thumb in my direction. "It's nice to meet you."

Katrina shook my hand. "I feel as if I know you," she said, narrowing her gaze. "Have we met?"

Ugh. A cold chill ran over my skin every time someone said something like this to me. Just when I was getting comfortable living my quiet life, a person mentioned they thought they recognized me. Fear tore through me and goosebumps pricked my skin.

"I own Sage Advice," I said while sweat dotted my brow. "Perhaps you've been in the store?"

"Yes, I have," she replied. "I was searching for a salve for my poor feet. The older I get, the more they ache. Dancing is so hard on the metatarsals."

I had no idea what part of the foot she spoke of, but I imagined after years of dance—especially ballet—the wear and tear would be significant. "Did you find what you were looking for?" I asked.

"No. I did purchase something, but it wasn't strong enough. I can't remember what it was now."

"Schedule a consultation with Annabelle," I said, pointing to her as she glided across the floor. "She's quite talented, and we're adding some CBD lines soon. They're very powerful."

Katrina glanced in the direction I pointed, then turned, her eyes wide with surprise. "I didn't see her when I came in to greet you!" she exclaimed. "What's she doing?"

"Practicing for the dance contest," I said.

"Ah," Katrina replied, turning back to us. "I'm afraid that may be off the table this year."

"That's too bad," I said. "Why is that?"

Katrina's face blanched. Her gaze jumped all around as though she'd find the answers somewhere.

"Is it because of the murder?" Gina whispered, leaning close to the dancer. "I heard one of your instructors was killed. Did she die here?"

Katrina's eyes closed for a brief moment, then she nodded. "How did you know?" she whispered. "We're trying to keep that under wraps."

"Just heard it through the grapevine," Gina said. "How did she die?"

"Strangled to death," Katrina mumbled. "It was awful. I found her."

"I'm sorry to hear that," I said. "Were you two close?"

She shook her head and sighed. "We used to be, but then I discovered she was pilfering my clients and giving them lessons outside the studio."

As I studied the graceful Katrina, I noted the strands of muscle rippling across her chest as she placed her hands on her hips and tilted her head to the side. "It's a shame what happened to the poor girl, though. Of course, I wouldn't wish death on anyone, despite such an awful betrayal."

"Of course," I said, smiling.

"Who do you think killed her?" Gina asked.

Katrina shrugged. "I heard they were blaming that cop she'd accused of sexual assault."

"Do you think he did it?" I asked.

"I have no idea. If I were to guess, I would say it was Brittney's boyfriend, Billy, though."

Gina and I traded glances. "Why do you say that?"

"Because it's always the boyfriend," Katrina replied. "Their relationship was rocky and volatile at best, and that's being kind. Besides, he left town almost immediately after she was killed. That seemed a little shady to me."

In my opinion, quite shady, indeed. And, Katrina was right. In most cases, murders were committed by people the victim knew. Billy murdering Brittney could've been a crime of passion, pure and simple.

"She also fought with Starlight," Katrina muttered, shaking her head. "I had to break up those two more than once."

"Physical altercations?" I asked, stunned, while trying to imagine Brittney in a fight. Granted, I hadn't known the woman except for a brief exchange when she worked in the sheriff's office, but she didn't seem like the fisticuffs type.

"Oh, yes," Katrina said. "They were like oil and water."

"What did they fight about?" Gina asked.

"Everything. About whose turn it was to clean the back room. A parking space. The last tiff was over Starlight's boyfriend. She said Brittney had been flirting with him over social media and sending him inappropriate pictures through private messenger." She shook her head. "It was a mess. I wanted to fire both of them, but qualified dance instructors are hard to find."

"Did you tell the police any of this?" I asked.

"Of course," Katrina replied. "But Sheriff Mallory seemed intent on the idea her deputy killed Brittney."

I recalled what Jordan had said: *I basically got Brittney fired, then she brought those charges against me. In order for them to go away, I killed her. It's neat and tidy for the sheriff and she won't have to do much work.*

It seemed Mallory had been willing to pin it on Jordan without even looking at any other possible leads.

"But let's get back to those dance lessons," Katrina said, lacing her long, delicate fingers in front of her. "What do you think about the thirty-day buffet package, as I like to call it?"

Based on Katrina's physique, she'd never bellied up to a buffet in her life, and I fought a snicker.

"That sounds good," Gina said. "We can try a little of everything and decide which one won't kill us."

Katrina paled again. "What does that mean?"

"She means, we're getting old and looking for a little exercise that won't hurt us or make us too sore," I said, trying to smooth things over. Gina's choice of wording had obviously upset the dance instructor.

A few girls—about ten years old—came in and kicked off their street shoes, then sat down on the floor to slip on their ballet slippers, chatting the whole time. Each wore identical pink leotards and white tights. They watched Annabelle intently as more girls flooded in.

"Where are all these kids coming from?" I asked, certain all of them weren't from Heywood proper.

"We're the premier studio in the area," Katrina said, beaming with pride. "They come from all over to learn from me. It's quite the honor."

We observed the girls another moment, then she said, "It's almost time for class. Let me get you that paperwork to fill out, as well as our adult class schedule."

As Katrina hurried out of the studio, Gina leaned over and said, "It's like she doesn't walk, but instead, she floats."

I nodded. We watched the dance instructor disappear through the arched doorway, then turned our attention back to Annabelle.

A few of the girls tentatively approached her and began copying her Michael Jackson moves, which Annabelle happily encouraged. After a few moments, other girls joined. Pretty soon, she had the whole class snapping, popping, and gliding across the floor. It could've been a Michael Jackson video.

"Oh, my gosh!" she yelled, jumping up and down. "You guys can be my backup dancers at the dance contest!"

The girls squealed in agreement and surrounded Annabelle as Katrina reentered. "Ladies, please gently stretch before we begin class!" she called. The girls scattered to the floor and barre and did as they were told, leaving Annabelle standing alone.

"She looks pretty sad over there by herself," Gina muttered.

I had to agree. Yes, rules and structure were important, but Katrina had really ruined a magical moment for Annabelle and the little ones.

"Here's the schedule," Katrina said, handing us each a few pieces of paper. "I've also included our waiver for you to sign and a general information sheet. I can't wait for you to find the joy of dance!"

Turning away from us, she clapped her hands three times and the girls all lined up against the wall, facing the same direction, their right leg pointed out in front of them, one arm holding the barre, the other set in first position. "Let's begin!" Katrina yelled.

"I think there's more joy in the bottom of a bottle of scotch," Gina muttered.

Annabelle walked over to us, her disappointment evident. "If I can get them to be my backup dancers, I'll win for sure," she whispered as we watched the class move through their warm-up.

"We better go," I said. "Gina and I need to figure out our classes."

"I don't know about that," Gina said while Annabelle slipped on her shoes.

When we were outside, I glared at my friend. "You can't back out now. You promised me you'd go to dance class with me!"

"And I will, but I think it's going to be a waste of time," Gina said. "I think Katrina did it."

"Why do you say that?" I asked, now intrigued about how she could come to that conclusion with the conversation we'd just had.

"Because Brittney was pilfering her clients," Gina replied, shrugging. "She was losing money. It's theft, and people will kill someone for taking money out of their pocket."

Interesting theory, and definitely one to keep in mind. "I still think we need to investigate further," I said. "If Katrina did kill Brittney, why would she admit her motive so easily?"

"Because Mallory already has Jordan nailed down as the murderer. At this point, what does it matter? Katrina is probably thinking the case is done."

Which was probably a correct assumption. The only thing left to do was arrest Jordan. Mallory was probably processing paperwork, dotting her I's and crossing her T's to make sure it was all legal.

"She's also throwing everyone else under the proverbial bus," Gina continued. "Brittney's boyfriend, Billy, another dancer... Who in the heck names their kid Starlight anyhow?"

Also great points. "We'll meet Starlight when we go to dance class," I said. "What ones do you want to start with?"

Gina groaned as we glanced at the schedule together.

"Waltzing," Annabelle said. "You guys should start with waltzing."

"I'd rather put my foot in a woodchipper," Gina grumbled.

"You're gross," Annabelle retorted, then pulled out her phone and glanced at the screen. "I need to get back to the store for a consultation, Sam. Do you want to ride with me?"

"Gina will drive me back," I said. "I'll see you in a bit."

As Annabelle walked across the parking lot, I returned my attention to the schedule. Starlight taught waltz. I pointed at the class. "We should start there. If Katrina thinks she could've killed Brittney in a crime of passion, we'll have to meet her."

Gina cursed again, then nodded. "What about the boyfriend?"

"Brittney's or Starlight's?" I asked.

"I guess both," Gina replied. "Both need to be questioned."

"Katrina mentioned Brittney's boyfriend, Billy, moved out of town shortly after her death. I wonder where he moved to?"

"Maybe Jordan would know," she said. "Perhaps he was privy to a few details before he got the sheriff's boot on his bottom."

Possibly, but did I want to ask him anything about the murder? Not really. I'd already decided I didn't want his input to taint my findings. But I may just need his help despite my wishes. I couldn't ask Mallory about any of it. She'd laugh in my face, tell me to mind my own business, and threaten me with prison for interfering with an investigation.

"Speaking of details… how did you know that Brittney had been killed at the dance studio?" I asked.

Gina shrugged. "I didn't. It was a lucky guess. When she said she was thinking of canceling the dance contest, there was only one thing I could think of that would make her want to do that."

"A murder."

"Right."

I turned my attention back to the schedule. One thing was certain—signing up for dance lessons had proved more beneficial than I could've imagined. We now had three good suspects: Katrina, Starlight, and Brittney's boyfriend, Billy.

At this point, all we needed to do was get close enough to question the three, and waltzing lessons with Starlight seemed to be the easiest way to weasel our way in and do so.

# CHAPTER 7

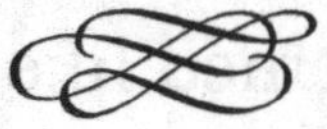

THE NEXT AFTERNOON, I stood in front of my closet for what seemed like a ridiculous amount of time. What did one wear to waltzing classes? Surely, I was overthinking the question. Why didn't I just pull out my leggings and sweatshirt?

Glancing at the paperwork from the studio again, I noted there wasn't any direction on this question. Yet, I felt a dress may be in order. I mean, we were going to be waltzing. I'd never seen anyone do so in workout gear, but then again, I didn't pay much attention to the waltzing world.

With a curse, I grabbed my leggings and sweatshirt. If I was dressed wrong, I'd know it immediately and make changes for the next class, hoping there wouldn't be one.

I hurried down the stairs to the back workroom where I found Annabelle hunched over her tinctures and capsules. Her eighties vibe was strong with what seemed like four hundred silver bracelets tinkling up and down her forearm and her Boy George t-shirt, acid-washed jeans, and bold eye makeup. Watching her for a moment, I admired her dedication to her craft… and the fact she allowed me to do ridiculous things like take waltzing lessons in the hopes of finding a killer.

"I'm leaving," I said quietly. "I'll be back shortly."

"Have a good time," she said. "I'll take care of any customers."

"Thanks a lot, Annabelle."

She stretched her arms over her head. "We have to make sure your boyfriend doesn't go to prison."

I shot her a glare. "He's not my boyfriend."

"Right," she said, winking. "Because you don't date. Heard it a million times, Sam."

For a second, I debated arguing with her and trying to explain my relationship with Jordan. Then, I decided not to bother because I really couldn't label it. We were close friends, but sometimes I did feel something else just below the surface. I always made sure to squash those thoughts and feelings because the last thing I needed was a man in my life. The betrayal by my former husband didn't allow for it. I probably should get over that, but I found it difficult to put behind me.

With a sigh, I grabbed my bag and headed out into the spring day. I loved this time of year—a period of fresh starts and renewals. Maybe I should apply that to my own life and let go of the past—concentrate on my big, bright future.

I walked down the street toward the dance studio. When my phone rang, I pulled it out of my bag. Jordan. Shoving it back into the big abyss, I debated returning the six phone calls he'd made since yesterday. I didn't want him involved or tainting my findings into who murdered Brittney, but at the same time, I'd probably have to speak to him to uncover important information. For now, he'd stay connected to my voicemail and I'd hope I hadn't angered him too much when we finally touched base.

Gina waited outside Groove and Go Dance for me. I waved and smiled, noting that she'd opted for leggings and a sweatshirt as well. She flipped me the bird, then gave me a hug.

"Did you fill out all your paperwork?" I asked.

Gina nodded.

"Let's do this," I said, yanking open the door.

Once again, the studio was quiet. A woman I didn't recognize entered the large area through the arched doorway.

"That must be Starlight," Gina whispered.

"Hello! Hello!" she greeted us, smiling. In her twenties, she wasn't as slim as Katrina, but she did have the same graceful walk. Brown hair flowed around her shoulders and she wore a black leotard with matching tights and a yellow ballet skirt that hung to her shins. I noted she also wore shoes with a slight heel. Maybe tap shoes?

"Hi," Gina muttered. "We're here for the waltzing class."

"Of course!" she exclaimed. "I'm Starlight! Welcome! Do either of you have any questions for me before the rest of the students arrive?"

I had a few questions, namely, how she ended up with a name like Starlight.

"No, I don't think so," I said.

"Great! And do you have your signed waivers?"

Gina and I each gave her our papers. "Perfect," she said, glancing over them. "Follow me to the back room."

"Should we take off our shoes?" I asked.

Starlight shook her head. "No. You'll need them for class. Although, it would've been better if you had shoes with a little heel instead of sneakers, but we'll work around that."

We trailed behind Starlight through the archway where we found another studio the same as the main one, but smaller. She pointed at a bench in the corner. "You can leave your bags there." Turning away from us, she hurried over to her phone and purse sitting on a small table on the other side of the room.

We walked over to the bench and sat down while I tried to figure out the best way to bring up the murder.

"So, I heard a dancer here died," Gina said.

Okay, then. Leave it to Gina to get the conversation started. I'd never use the term 'subtle' to describe her. She said what she wanted, when she wanted. I appreciated her directness, but even now, sometimes it caught me up short.

I shot her a glare, then studied Starlight as she glanced over her shoulder at us. A swath of emotions crossed her face, ranging from sadness to anger, and landing there. "Yes, you're correct. Brittney was her name. She was murdered." Her purse tipped over and the contents scattered. Whispering a curse, she squatted to pick them up.

"Oh, wow. How did that happen?" Gina asked, standing and approaching Starlight. "Were you two close?"

I followed, surprised the dancer was actually answering Gina's questions and also at the amount of stuff she carried in her purse. I picked up a tube of lipstick, a silver star-shaped barrette, and two feminine hygiene products then handed them back to her. She smiled as she shoved everything back in the bag and set it on the table.

"At one time, but if anyone knew how to burn a bridge, it was Brittney," Starlight said, shaking her head. "That girl poured gasoline on every relationship she had and lit a match to it."

"We heard through the grapevine you two fought a lot," I hedged, hoping I hadn't taken my probing too far.

"Oh, yes. That wasn't a secret," Starlight replied. "She tried to steal my boyfriend, and she never carried her weight around the studio. Everything was done with little effort, and then when Katrina would say something about the shoddy job, Brittney would blame me."

"I'm sorry to hear about that," Gina said. "We heard she was killed here."

The dancer nodded and glanced around.

Making sure we were alone, perhaps? "She was. Katrina found her in—"

Footsteps and voices sounded from the front studio and seconds later, three couples came in—two elderly and one young—all grinning and laughing. They obviously knew each other.

"We need to get class started," Starlight said, waving and smiling at them.

"Can we talk to you after?" I asked.

"Sure." She stepped into the middle of the room and clapped her hands three times, just as Katrina had done. "Welcome, everyone! Let's get waltzing!"

Gina and I traded glances when the couples lined up holding each other in a dancer's embrace. I hadn't given any thought to the fact this was a couples' class. I turned to Gina. "Do you want to lead?"

"Fine," she muttered.

"I'm going to go over our steps for our newest dancers, starting with the Box Step," Starlight said. "Remember, our rhythm is one, two three. Leads, you start with your left foot. Left forward, right forward. Right foot back, left foot meets it. Partners, it's the opposite for you. Everyone ready?"

The music began, a classical number I didn't

recognize. Starlight raised her hands in front of her, as if she had a partner. "And, begin!" she shouted, stepping forward.

Taking a deep breath, I also stepped forward… directly onto Gina's foot.

She hissed and swore as the other couples danced around us. "Your *left* foot, Sam! *Left!*"

"I'm sorry," I muttered. I'd always been horrible at figuring out my right versus left, unless I concentrated on it.

After a few more attempts, Gina and I finally got the hang of it, and we waltzed along with everyone else.

"This isn't so bad," I whispered.

"One, two three, one two three," she muttered back. "Don't break my concentration."

When the song ended, the other couples bowed to each other, all smiles and laughter. "Well, done, everyone!" Starlight yelled. "You looked beautiful!"

"What do you think their story is?" I asked, pointed at the younger people.

"Wedding," Gina said. "They're practicing for the wedding dance. The other people… they're here reliving their youth."

"And now on to the forward progressive!"

Starlight said, then gave directions and a little demonstration.

"We're never going to get this one." Gina sighed.

As the music began and the other couples danced, Gina and I gave it a try, but she ended up on the floor after kicking my shin. Starlight rushed over but I waved her off. "We're going to sit this one out," I said, pulling Gina to her feet.

"We'll stick around until the end and then talk to Starlight a bit more," I said as we sat down on the bench and I rubbed my shin. "You really nailed my leg."

"Sorry about that," she muttered. "Instead of going through all this misery, maybe it wouldn't be a bad idea to let Jordan rot in prison."

I shot her a glare, knowing she was kidding. Well, maybe only partially.

After class, Starlight said her goodbyes to the other couples, then glided over to see us. "Are you two okay?" she asked.

I nodded. "I don't think waltzing is for us."

"Probably not," she said. "You may enjoy the Zumba classes, though."

"Earlier you were telling us about Brittney's murder," Gina ventured.

Starlight sighed and nodded. "Yes. Katrina

found her in the other small studio. She'd been strangled with a bunch of toe shoe ribbons woven together. Whoever killed her had put a lot of thought into it. Katrina said they were braided together to form a very strong rope."

Jordan certainly hadn't mentioned that. And as bad as it sounded, I admired the killer's ingenuity. I was a little upset that after decades on the soap opera, *As The Years Turn*, the writers and I hadn't come up with that method of killing someone for my character on the show, Cassie. And here I thought we'd considered every which way to end someone's life.

"If you had to guess who killed her, who would you say did it?" I asked.

Starlight shrugged. "I honestly have no idea. I hope it's no one who works here."

I'd been under the impression Katrina owned the studio and Starlight and Brittney were the employees. Were there more?

"Is there someone else employed here?" I asked.

"We have a couple people that come in to volunteer. They aren't paid." She glanced around the room again, then whispered, "Brittney was stealing clients from Katrina, though, and she was very angry about it when she found out. When they got into it, I wouldn't have been surprised if Katrina became physical with her."

"It sounds like you think Katrina could've had something to do with it," Gina said, her voice low.

"It's a possibility," Starlight muttered. "If Katrina did kill Brittney, it was for stealing her clients. Revenge, I guess you could say."

I picked up my bag and stood. "Thank you for the class and for your time," I said. "Gina and I were curious about her death, and you've provided us with a lot of information we didn't know."

"Why do you want all these details?" Starlight asked. "Here I am running my mouth and I don't even know you."

Yes, why, indeed. I didn't want people to figure out we were trying to solve the murder.

"I'm a writer," Gina said. "I'm doing some legwork to see if I want to write a book on this murder."

"Ah, I see," Starlight said.

"But our conversation stays between us," I said.

"Okay, good. I don't want Katrina to know I was gossiping about her."

"If you think there's a possibility Katrina

killed Brittney, are you afraid to continue working here?" I asked.

She shook her head. "I keep my nose clean and do my job. Besides, now that I really think about it, it was probably Brittney's boyfriend or that cop who assaulted her."

"Why do you say that?" Gina asked.

"Well, Billy was a jerk, and that cop was under investigation for what he did. If I were in his shoes, I'd want my accuser to disappear, too."

# CHAPTER 8

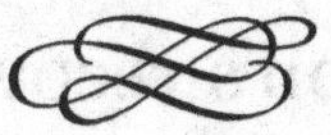

I RETURNED to the store to find Annabelle speaking with a customer while one waited at the counter, ready to be checked out. After hurrying behind the cash register, I smiled and was shocked to see it was Mrs. Pugh waiting for me.

"Hello," I said, my discomfort growing with each passing second. I had sent her husband to prison for murdering Gina's ex-husband, Ralph, who was found dead in Gina's store, File It Away.

"Hello, Sam," she said, glaring at me with hatred. "I'd like this lavender tincture, please. I'm sure you can understand that my stress levels are through the roof trying to run the farm on my own. *Without my husband.*"

Translation: her stress levels were my fault.

I hadn't enjoyed leading Jordan to her house to elicit a confession, but I also hadn't wanted Gina to spend the rest of her life in jail. After ringing her up and processing her credit card, I slipped the bottle into one of our Sage Advice bags. "How's your son's recovery going?" I asked, hoping the drug addict had stayed clean to help his mom with the farm.

"So far, so good," she muttered, taking the bag from me. "Thank you."

Guilt washed through me as she walked out. I'd taken their family from a bad position and only made it worse. However, I also hated the idea of someone going down for something they didn't do. Been there, done that and loathed my dead husband for it. I could never have allowed it to happen to Gina.

With a sigh, I checked out another customer, then wiped down the counter.

"How was dance class?" Annabelle asked.

"About how you would expect."

"Who ended up on the floor?" she teased. "Was it you or Gina?"

I pulled up my pantleg and showed her the huge bruise forming on my shin. "Right after she did this to me, she went down."

Annabelle laughed and shook her head. "I almost wish I could've seen it, but I would've been so embarrassed for you."

"How are things going here?" I asked, glancing around the now-empty store. "Everything okay?"

"Of course," she replied. "Now tell me what you learned."

I went over our conversation with Starlight in great detail because I knew a lot of times, Annabelle thought things through a little differently than the average person.

"It's interesting that both she and Katrina are willing to throw each other under the proverbial bus," Annabelle said. "And both also pointed the finger at Brittney's boyfriend."

"And don't you think it's strange that he skipped town right after she was killed?" I asked. "That seems really suspicious to me."

She nodded. "Same. It definitely makes him, like, look guilty. Do we know where he went?"

"No. I have no idea." But Jordan probably would, which was another reason for me to contact him.

"Strangulation with ballet ribbons would require a lot of strength," Annabelle mused. "We're definitely looking for someone strong."

"I can't rule anyone out with those standards," I said. "Katrina literally has muscles rippling beneath her skin. Starlight isn't any wilting flower, either. Both are physically capable of the crime, especially if it was done with hatred in their heart."

"But are they mentally capable?" Annabelle asked. "That's the question. If Brittney was stealing clients from Katrina and also attempting to, like, move in on Starlight's boyfriend... I would think they'd be able to kill her. It would just depend on how mad Brittney made each of them."

My phone rang. Even before glancing at the screen, I knew it was Jordan again. I sent it to voicemail and then shoved it back into my pocket.

"You're going to have to talk to him at some point," Annabelle said.

So she realized I was dodging him.

"He asked you to help him and now you're ignoring him, Sam. It's not very nice."

"I just want to make sure he stays away from the investigation," I said. "I don't want his input." But I should've been smart enough to question him about the case before agreeing to find the killer. Most likely, he had details from police reports he may have seen before being put on leave.

That was stupid of me, to say the least. I jumped in with both feet without proper preparation.

"Why don't you want his input?" she asked. "It's his life on the line. I think he should, like, have a say in everything. He may even be a big help."

Or a hindrance, if he was lying to me and he really did kill Brittney. As much as I wanted to believe he didn't, I still had my doubts. Trust issues for the win.

Did I tell Annabelle about the case in his past that mirrored the current one? As I debated how much to share, the front door opened and a man walked in wearing jeans, a white t-shirt and a flannel jacket. Sporting a smile, he looked to be in his thirties with a mess of black hair and a thick, matching beard. My contractor.

"Hey, Mike," I said. I'd given the go-ahead on the deck, and he said he'd start the legwork.

"Sam, listen, we have a problem," he said, approaching the counter.

"What's that?" I asked, crossing my arms over my chest, not liking that we'd run into issues before the first nail had been hit.

"I went to grab the permits for the deck, and there's an environmental note on the property."

"What does that, like, even mean?" Annabelle asked.

"It means that a citizen has shared concerns that building this deck will lead to environmental problems."

"How does that work?" I asked. "Almost every single store has one, except mine."

Mike shrugged. "I know, and I tried to explain that to the people at City Hall, but they take citizens' concerns about building very seriously. There's going to have to be an environmental study done to make sure the impact will be minimal."

Stunned, I took a seat on a stool. How in the world could Sage Advice be singled out like that?

"Who's the complainant?" Annabelle asked.

"Let me look," Mike replied, pulling out his phone. "I actually made a note of his name."

As he scrolled through the phone, my anger rose, flushing my cheeks as I dug into my palms with my short nails. I'd made a few people mad by sending their loved ones to jail for murders, but would they go to this extent for revenge? Mrs. Pugh had been a little sarcastic toward me, although still not outwardly mean. But if looks could kill, I'd be dead. Was this her way of getting a dig at me?

Or perhaps it was Catherine, Bonnie's daughter. I hadn't seen or heard from her in months, but she was a vengeful person. Bonnie had left the store to me, not her, and maybe this was her retribution? Strangling the store's growth?

But wait. Mike had said *his* name. A man.

Charlie Tupper immediately came to mind. His wife, Doreen, had died before she'd gone to trial for murdering Bonnie. I'd been invited to her funeral, and Charlie and I had made our peace… or so I thought.

"Gerald Butte," Mike said, then glanced up at me.

"Are you kidding me?!" Annabelle shrieked as I sat stunned. It was one thing for him to harass us, but for him to actually interfere with expanding the business… I couldn't believe he'd stoop so low.

But he'd mentioned time and again that he wanted Sage Advice closed. If he couldn't shut us down, he'd try to keep us from growing.

"Do you know him?" Mike asked.

"We do," I replied as a hot flash tore through me. Thanks to Annabelle's herbal remedies, it had been a while since I'd had one so severe, and I couldn't help wonder if it was anger, not menopause. I gave him a brief recounting of my history with Butte. "When did he share his concerns with City Hall?"

"It was about two months ago," Mike replied.

I glanced over at Annabelle. "How in the world did he discover our plans?"

"Who knows?" she said, shrugging. "Someone could've overheard us talking and passed along the information. This is a small town and sometimes, there's not a lot to discuss except rumors and other people's business."

A sickly feeling settled in my gut and I wasn't sure if it was fury or plain old disgust at the fact Butte had done this.

"What does an environmental study involve?" I asked.

Mike shrugged. "Money, mainly. I know a guy who works for an independent company out of Phoenix. I can convince him to come up and do some fishing, and he can get it done then."

"Let's do it," I said, slapping my palm on the counter.

"It's going to put you over budget," Mike said. "Not by a lot, but it's going to cost you."

The longer I simmered in the news of Butte's doings, the more I wanted that deck built. "I don't care," I said. "That deck is going up. I'm serving tea on it this summer if it's the last thing I do."

I'd figure out the money later. We could bump our advertising budget a bit in hopes it paid off. Or I'd sell my bone marrow. Too bad I probably didn't have any good eggs left. Even though I came from pretty poor stock, they may be valuable simply because of who I used to be before arriving in Heywood.

"Okay," Mike said. "Let me get my buddy on the phone and I'll let you know when the inspection will take place."

"Thanks, Mike," I replied. "I appreciate it. And the sooner, the better. Okay?"

"Yes, ma'am." He gave us a quick salute and exited the store.

"I can't believe that old jerk did this," Annabelle muttered. Glancing over at her, I realized she was seething—even more so than me.

"It's okay," I said. "We'll get the inspection and move forward. It's just a hiccup."

She shook her head. "He needs to pay for this."

I sighed as a headache formed behind my eyes. "What are you going to do?" I asked. "Slash his tires?"

"That's something Bonnie would've done. No, I won't do that."

Her jaw worked as she stared at the front door and my stomach flipped and flopped. When Gina had been in jail, Annabelle had broken into Ralph's home and stolen a bunch of money. He'd owed Gina for years of back child support and Annabelle had wanted to make it right.

I worried for what she had planned now. "Maybe it's best just to let things lie," I said, laying my hand over her fist sitting in her lap. "Don't do anything rash."

She narrowed her gaze and snorted. "That's not something Cassie would say. She'd get her revenge."

I didn't bother to mention Cassie had been a character on television who did a lot of things for ratings that wouldn't fly in real life.

"Trust me, Sam," she muttered. "I'm not going to do anything rash."

I didn't believe her but decided to let it go. I had to get back to working on finding out who killed Brittney. Perhaps Annabelle would cool down a bit and start thinking rationally.

Based on the gleam in her eye, I doubted it.

# CHAPTER 9

I'D SIGNED up Gina and me for a late-afternoon Zumba class the next day. After tending to the store all day, I went upstairs and slipped on a pair of leggings and a t-shirt. Catnip studied me from the bed, his critical stare raking me over from head to toe. Sometimes, I could ignore it, but today I found it disconcerting.

"Are you judging me?" I asked, sitting down and pulling on my sneaker. "I would appreciate it if you didn't. I know I've put on a little weight, Catnip."

He meowed, as if in agreement, then stretched out and shut his eyes. "It's not like you couldn't stand to lose a few, too, you know," I mumbled. "That's the kettle calling the pot black." Leaning over, I gave him a quick kiss, then headed back down to walk over to Groove and Go Dance.

"Have fun!" Annabelle called as I exited the building. "Shake that booty, Sam!"

I was more concerned about hurting myself than my booty-shaking.

As I walked, I shifted my gaze from one side of the street to the other. Jordan had called twice during the day, and I half-expected him to ambush me to talk. I'd decided I'd hunt him down after dance class. There were too many details I didn't know about the crime and I hoped he could give me some answers.

When I arrived at the dance studio, I waited outside for Gina. After a few minutes, I called, hoping she wasn't going to blow me off. I cursed when she didn't answer. Seconds later, my phone rang.

"Sam, I'm not going to make it," Gina said breathlessly. "There's a dog that's hurt... I'm working with some other volunteers to try to catch him to get him to the vet."

Oh no. I never understood how Gina worked as a dog rescuer. Just hearing about the distressed animal wrenched my heart. She dealt with it day in and day out.

"Where are you?" I asked.

"I... I don't even know. Out in the middle of nowhere. Gotta go."

Disappointment railed through me. Of course, the injured dog was more important than this stupid dance class, but it was always easier to make a fool of myself with a friend than all by my lonesome.

I stood outside, debating whether to take the class. We could always go the next day. Just as I was about to walk back to Sage Advice, I heard two women yelling inside Groove and Go. I opened the door slowly, then stepped in. The front studio was empty and the voices carried from the arched doorway to my right. No need for me to enter any further. Their voices were so loud, I heard everything just fine.

"I'm sorry you were taken for a ride!" Katrina yelled. "But we have no responsibility to reimburse you!"

"She worked here!" the woman screamed. "It was a year's worth of dance classes!"

"Yes, she did. And she told you that she would give you lessons outside of the studio. You gave her your money to do so. I have nothing to do with her taking your money."

"But it was a year's worth of classes!" the woman yelled.

"Brittney is dead," Katrina said, her voice now calm. "I can't help you."

"She was ghosting me before she died," the customer said. "She took my money and didn't give me even one lesson!"

Katrina sighed. "I'm sorry she did that. She had no business taking my clients and making them her own. Yes, she stole from you, she stole from me, but she's dead now and there's nothing either one of us can do about how she wronged us."

"I know that, but you still should reimburse me!"

"There is nothing for me to atone for," Katrina said. "Absolutely nothing. You made a deal with the devil and now you have to pay the consequences, which, in this case, is the loss of your money. Perhaps you could sue her estate or something like that, but I'm not responsible for her actions."

"You were her employer! Of course you're responsible!"

"Yes, I was her employer, but she went behind my back and agreed to give you lessons outside my studio. She'd signed an agreement that she wouldn't do that, but she did. You agreed to the terms she laid out."

"Brittney got what she deserved!" the woman shouted. "But I thought you'd make it right!"

A moment later, the woman stomped toward me, coming from the arched doorway, her hands fisted at her sides. Her long brown hair flowed behind her almost like a cape. About my age, she glared at me as she approached. I opened the door for her and quickly followed her out.

"Excuse me," I called.

She turned. "What? What do you want?"

"I was wondering if we could talk for a minute about Brittney," I said. "I couldn't help but overhear your argument with Katrina."

"That woman should repay me for what Brittney did," she hissed. I watched in fascination as she grabbed a chunk of her hair and began braiding it. Her fingers moved swiftly as she continued her tirade. Right, left. Right, left. "It makes no sense to me. Brittney worked for her and that snot took my money. The woman got what she deserved. She's a lying thief."

I nodded absently as her eyes dilated. For a second, fear coursed through me and I stepped away. It was like witnessing someone coming completely unhinged or possessed.

"Did Brittney pull the same thing with you?" she asked.

"Y-yes," I lied. "She did. I was also hoping to get my money back."

I went down that path in hopes of the woman trusting me and sharing more of her story. Was she right in thinking Katrina owed her? No. It had been a side deal between Brittney and this woman. But I found her reasoning interesting.

"Do I know you?" she asked. "You look like that one actress. Don't tell me her name."

Her fingers continued working in her hair until she reached the end. Then she pulled it all apart and began again. Right, left. Right, left.

"Andie MacDowell!" she yelled, jumping up and down, her hair temporarily forgotten as she flailed her arms around. "I knew I'd remember her name!"

Immediately, she returned to her braiding. I stood stunned, unsure of what to say to her. Then I noted the strap to her bag was braided pieces of leather, and it definitely appeared handmade. The fact that Brittney had been killed with toe shoe ribbons woven together wasn't lost on me.

Finally, I cleared my throat. "So, why do you think Brittney deserved to die?"

"Because she's a liar and a thief. I already told you that. Listen up. Hear my words. I don't like repeating myself."

"Of course," I replied, smiling. "I'm sorry about that."

She held up a fist in front of her. "I'd like to wrap my fingers around her throat and squeeze the life out of her."

Oh, my. What was this? Mental illness? Drugs? Evil?

"What did you say your name was?" I asked.

"Gretchen Riley," she said.

"I'm Sam," I replied, sticking out my hand. "It's nice to meet someone else who had the same experience with Brittney as me."

"Did you want her dead, too?" she asked, taking my palm in hers.

"Well, I don't know about that, but I did want my money back."

Gretchen continued to work her hair. Was it some sort of tick or impulse? Did she even realize she was moving the strands? "Like I said, she got what she deserved."

We stood in silence for a moment as I studied her and attempted to answer my own questions.

"I've got to go," she said. "I'm going to be late for work."

"Where do you work at?" I asked.

She narrowed her gaze. "That's none of your business."

"I'm sorry," I replied, "I was just trying to be friendly."

"Just like Brittney," she mumbled, turning away from me.

I let out a long breath I didn't realize I'd been holding and tried to regroup my thoughts. Obviously, Gretchen liked to braid things, and she was very fast. She'd been acquainted with Brittney and held a big grudge against her. But was it enough to kill her?

If she was the killer, why walk around saying Brittney got what she deserved? Was she bragging about the fact she'd done it but hadn't been caught? Or was she innocent and simply sharing her anger?

Brittney had been killed inside the studio after hours, so whoever had murdered her had to have had access a normal customer didn't. Gretchen didn't qualify there as far as I knew. Or had Brittney not only stolen Katrina's customers, but also used her dance studio to give lessons after hours?

I went inside and found Katrina standing near the front door, her arms crossed over her chest. "Good afternoon, Sam," she said, her voice cold.

"Hi, Katrina," I greeted her. "How are things going?"

"Well, I didn't mean to overhear your conversation with Gretchen, but I did. I was wondering, did you just lie to the woman or did Brittney take money from you and never give you any dance lessons?"

Dang it. Being caught lying was never a good look for anyone. "No," I replied. "I was just curious to hear her story and I wanted to bond with her a bit."

"Why? Brittney is dead. Can't we all let the woman rest in peace? Why does she keep on living in our conversations and thoughts?"

Brittney had been dead just short of two weeks. Why wouldn't people want to discuss her? "Well, she apparently affected a lot of people's lives and some of them, not in a good way." Surely, there had to be people out there who loved and missed the woman. Everyone had someone who loved them, right?

Katrina sighed and placed her hands on her waist as she glared at me. "I'm not one for gossip, but I'll say this. Brittney was like a cancer on this studio and in my life. Chaos ensued wherever she went. She took advantage of people, like poor Gretchen there, and didn't think twice about it."

The dancer may have a point. She'd also accused Jordan of sexual assault, moved in on Starlight's boyfriend, caused problems in the studio, and stolen clients from Katrina. So maybe she was just a horrible human.

"You're asking a lot of questions about Brittney," Katrina hedged. "Why? Are you some type of reporter?"

I shook my head. "No. My friend, Gina, is a writer and she's considering doing a book on the killing. We're just trying to get background information before she makes her decision." Thank goodness Gina had the talent of lying under pressure.

"Okay, interesting," Katrina said. "I was wondering what your story is."

"I am interested in dance lessons," I replied, hating the lie came so easily to me.

"It makes sense now," she said, nodding. "As for Gretchen, I've always felt bad for her. She's not right mentally, but she loved being in the studio and is a strong dancer. I gave her odd jobs around the place so she could spend time here in exchange for a discount on dance lessons. To have Brittney take advantage of her like she did breaks my heart, but I'm also not going to go out of pocket and repay Gretchen for Brittney's scams."

Wait a minute. Odd jobs? "What did Gretchen do for you here?" I asked.

Katrina shrugged. "Some cleaning. Filing. Things like that."

"Did that mean she had access to the studio after hours?"

"Yes, she did."

Well, Gretchen obviously had a thing for braiding, she had a bone to pick with Brittney and she had access to the studio after hours.

Had I just discovered the killer?

# CHAPTER 10

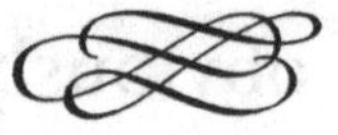

AFTER MY UTTER failure at Zumba, I exited the studio and wiped the sweat from my brow, then pulled my curls up into a frizzy ponytail. Zumba was not for me and I was going to feel it in the morning. My knees ached and I may have thrown out my back. Give me mindless jogging or a good, swift walk any day.

I pulled out my phone and dialed Jordan. After one ring, it went straight to voicemail. He seemed to now be playing my game. Glancing up and down the street, I tried to figure out where he could be. He wasn't at the station, that was certain. But was he at home? If so, I couldn't walk there—he lived too far out of town. There was however one place I could check, somewhere I knew he liked to be, especially when he needed to unwind. And if there was a time he needed relaxation, it was now.

As I hurried down the street toward the restaurant, On the River, I tried dialing him again. No answer. I shoved the phone in my pocket, thankful for the cool evening air. Maybe my sweat would dry before I reached my destination and I'd be able to walk the knot out of my back.

I pulled open the door and the scents of fresh baked goods and cooking spices engulfed me. Sally, the owner, may serve what one would call "bar food," but she also used the local farms to source her vegetables, meat and herbs, which resulted in the freshest, most delicious grub I'd ever tasted. I glanced around the log-cabin-like space in search of Jordan and found him in a booth in the rear near the front windows, his back to me. I'd recognize that shoulder span and thick, salt and pepper hair anywhere. Just as I was about to walk over to him, Sally approached and waved. Thin with a beak-like nose, wide eyes and long brown hair, she reminded me a bit of an ostrich.

"Hi, Sam," she said. "How's it going?"

"Good," I replied. "I was looking for Jordan."

She pointed over to him. "He's having some coffee and a vegetable omelet."

"Oh, nice," I said, suddenly famished. "Can I get one as well?"

"Sure," she said. "Just be aware he's in an awful mood."

Being accused of murder could do that to a person. "I'll be careful," I said. "Hopefully he won't bite."

She laughed, turned, and made her way to the kitchen as I walked toward the man, then sat down across from him.

Our gazes locked for a second and he arched an eyebrow. "I see you're acknowledging my existence now," he said.

"Sorry about that," I said, the smell of Sally's amazing food wafting over to me and causing my stomach to rumble. I realized I hadn't eaten since this morning and the Zumba class had taken a lot out of me. I couldn't wait to scrape the plate.

Jordan continued, "I was coming to the conclusion that you think I killed Brittney and don't want anything to do with me." He picked up his cup of coffee and sipped it while glaring at me over the rim.

"Well, I have some doubts," I said.

"Doubts that I'm innocent?" he asked incredulously. "Are you kidding me, Sam?"

I sighed and closed my eyes for a moment, wishing I hadn't shared my thoughts. When I opened them, he stared at me angrily. "Jordan, I'm sorry, but there is the issue that this case has a pretty strong resemblance to what happened in Chicago."

"Fine," he said. "I'll take care of everything. I'm sorry I asked for your help."

"Hold up a second," I said, placing my hand over his. "I didn't say I wasn't going to help you. Only that I had some doubts."

He shook his head. "I can't have you hesitant in believing that I didn't kill Brittney."

Sally approached and set down my omelet and coffee, her smile slowly fading. "I don't like the tension over here," she said. "You two are usually so happy when you come in. What gives?"

I glared at Jordan but remained quiet. It wasn't my place to announce what had caused the turmoil at our table.

Finally, he broke our stare down, smiled, and looked up at Sally. "It's nothing, Sally. Thanks for your concern."

She furrowed her brow and nodded uncertainly but left us alone.

Jordan turned back to me, his cheeks tinged red with anger. "If you think for a second that I killed Brittney, then please just leave."

I should've kept my trust issues to myself.

Lowering his voice, he poked his fork in my direction. "You and I have been getting together a lot, Sam. I told you about a time in my life that almost destroyed me. I laid it all out for you, and this is what I get? You think I actually killed that girl?" He shook his head.

A small part of me wanted to get up and walk out, let him deal with the mess. But when it came down to it, I really did want to help him. I needed to prove to myself I wasn't a terrible judge of character, and that I hadn't hitched my cart to another bad horse, like my dead husband had been.

"Jordan, I have a few questions about the case… stuff I should've asked you before I even agreed to help you out."

"What?" he sighed, his fork clattering to his plate. "What does it matter if there's a chance you think I did it?"

"Tell me about the crime scene," I said. "Brittney was found in Groove and Go, right?"

He nodded, his anger visibly deflating. "Yes.

Strangled to death with some ribbons braided together."

"I understand that Katrina found her?"

"Correct."

"When? What time of day?" I asked.

"In the morning when she went in to open. Katrina found Brittney laid out in the middle of the floor, spread-eagle, with the ribbons around her neck."

That jived with what she'd shared with me, so at least someone was telling the truth.

"Did you ever speak to her yourself, or was that just in the reports?" I asked.

"No, I did talk to her. I was first on the scene. She was pretty shaken up. Mallory arrived shortly after I did, though, and told me to get lost."

"Why?"

"Because of the sexual assault allegations by the victim."

I noted the way he spoke of the case as if he were describing something that didn't directly involve him.

"Did you believe Katrina?" I asked. "Or do you think it was all an act?"

He narrowed his gaze and stared at the table for a long moment before answering. "I was convinced then that she was telling me the truth, but now, I'm not so sure."

"Why is that?"

"I don't know," Jordan replied. "Just a feeling, I suppose. Or maybe it's because I'm the main suspect and I'd give just about anything to have the target off my back."

Fair enough, and completely understandable.

"Did you guys ever interview someone named Gretchen Riley?" I asked.

He shook his head. "Not that I recall. Why?"

I told him about my run in with her and the fight with Katrina.

"That's interesting," he said. "Especially about the braiding tic, or whatever that is."

"I thought so as well. Is there any way I can see pictures of the crime scene?"

"Mallory cut off all my computer access. I can't get into the files."

"Can you call in a favor? Maybe another deputy could send them to you?"

He shook his head slowly. "I don't know, Sam. That's a big ask."

"Yes, but I'm attempting to picture it. It's not like I enjoy looking at dead bodies. I'm just trying to help."

"I'll see what I can do," he sighed. "No promises, though."

"That's fair," I said, taking a sip of coffee and changing the trajectory of conversation. "In order to strangle someone, strength is required, right?"

Jordan nodded. "Yes, it is."

"I don't know if Gretchen has it, but Katrina and Starlight sure do. They're both powerhouses with all the dancing they've done throughout their lives."

He nodded and pursed his lips. "I agree, but I was always curious about the boyfriends."

"Plural?" I asked. "Brittney had more than one?"

"Not that I know of," he said. "But I was referring to Starlight's boyfriend, too. I never got to interview him."

"Why would he be considered a suspect?" I asked, now confused. "I didn't know he could be involved in this."

Jordan shrugged. "Brittney and Starlight fought a lot. From my understanding, a couple of times it became physical. He made threats against Brittney. Told her to stop hitting on him and leave Starlight alone or he'd make her sorry."

"I hadn't heard about the threats," I replied. "How did you find that out?"

"Starlight told me."

Why hadn't she shared this piece of information with me?

"And no one bothered to ask him about it?"

He shook his head. "Not that I'm aware of. I was put on leave shortly after we interviewed her."

This new information put a spin on the investigation. I'd been thinking it was one of the women associated with the studio, but there were other avenues that needed to be explored.

"What about Billy?" I asked. "Brittney's boyfriend?"

"I spoke to him the day after she died, then he left town. He was devastated—really broken up."

"And you believed his reaction wasn't an act? Katrina said their relationship was volatile."

"I don't know about that, but he loved her." Jordan shrugged and slowly spun his coffee cup. "I still think he's innocent. I've seen some people trying to fake grief, but it's difficult to do. There's an element to it that's so profound, so deep, it's almost impossible to find unless you're in the throes of it."

Not sure about that. I'd seen some amazing performances in my time in Hollywood and gave a few I'd been proud of. Could grief be faked? Yes.

Was there a small element missing in the acting? Maybe?

We sat quietly for a long moment as I digested this new information and finished off my omelet.

"The funeral's tomorrow," Jordan said, "at the town church. If I was still in uniform, I'd attend. But I think it's a bad idea for me to be there since I'm the number one suspect."

"I agree," I muttered. "I'd feel uneasy being there as well."

When my boss, Bonnie, had died, there'd been a small service for family only. I'd gone and hid under a pew so I could hear what was being said. Luck had been on my side that day, and I wasn't found out. I didn't think I could get away with it twice.

But I could sit in the parking lot to check out who came to pay their respects to Brittney. Maybe even ambush a few people and see if they dropped any clues to the murder. "Will Billy be there?" I asked.

"I have no idea, Sam. My guess is yes, but you never know."

"I'd love to talk to him," I muttered. "I think I'll go stake it out and see who shows up."

"What do you mean, stake it out?" Jordan asked. "Are you going to crash a funeral?"

I shook my head. "No. I'm not going into the church. Just hang out in the parking lot in Annabelle's car and see if I can talk to Billy and anyone else who piques my interest."

"Bad idea. It could be dangerous."

"What does he look like?" I asked, ignoring his warning.

"Tall, lanky guy with blond hair. About thirty. I don't think this is a good idea, though," he insisted.

With a sigh, I said, "Do you want my help or not?"

"Of course I do," he replied. "But what I don't want is to see you hurt. If the killer is there tomorrow, they could feel threatened with you around. You're already asking questions."

"Under the guise that Gina's writing a book about Brittney's murder," I said. "I don't think I'm on anyone's radar."

"Very clever," he muttered, smiling at me for the first time since I sat down. "Actually, sort of brilliant."

"I thought so, too. Wish I could take credit for it, but I can't. That girl can really think on her feet. Did I tell you we're also taking dance lessons?"

Jordan arched an eyebrow and failed miserably at trying to hide a smile while giving off all sorts of George Clooney vibes. "No, you didn't mention that. I wish I could see it."

"I'm glad you can't," I said. "I just finished a Zumba class."

"I was wondering why it looked like you ran a marathon. How did that go?"

"I'm not Zumba material," I said, stretching my arms above my head, my muscles aching. "My body is already in protest."

Jordan snickered and shook his head. "It's good to see you, Sam."

"I'm sorry about ghosting you like that," I said. "I just needed some space to try to figure stuff out on my own."

"I understand. I hate you having doubts about my innocence, though."

How did I explain my trust issues without diving into my past? Maybe it was time for me to level with Jordan on who I really was and what brought me to Heywood. But not tonight.

"I've got to go," I said, reaching for my bag. "Let me get some money for my food."

"I'll take care of it," he said. "My treat."

"Thanks. That's sweet of you."

"It's the least I can do, Sam. I appreciate your help."

As I exited the restaurant, I couldn't help but wonder if Jordan was trying to be extra nice in order for me to think of him as innocent, or if that was just his nature.

You'd think I'd have that worked out by now.

# CHAPTER 11

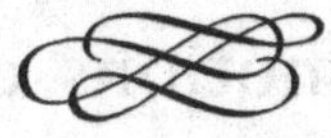

THE NEXT DAY I sat in Annabelle's car in the parking lot of the church, an old, stone building that had been constructed when Heywood had first been discovered. It had originally been a Catholic church but was now non-denominational. Minister Paul, who held similarities to a younger Paul Rudd, propped open the large wooden doors then disappeared back inside. I'd arrived early to get a prime spot from where I could see everyone coming and going without being noticed.

As I waited for the funeral attendees to arrive, my mind kept wandering back to Gretchen and her braiding. Right, left, right, left. The fact Brittney had been strangled with braided ballet ribbons definitely cast a long shadow of guilt on the woman. She had motive. She had access to the studio. And the braids were a dead giveaway.

But did she have the strength? I honestly didn't know, but if I were a betting woman, I'd say no. However, emotions could bring out extreme physical abilities in people. Mothers had lifted cars off their children. If she'd been angry enough, which it seemed she most certainly could have been, perhaps she'd found the strength to kill Brittney.

During my time in Hollywood, I'd had my hair braided many times. My long-time stylist, a lovely woman my age named Paula, had created all sorts of intricate designs for my red-carpet appearances. Since my curls needed to be straightened and then braided, it had taken hours each time. I'd never been disappointed with the results. The thing that struck me about Paula was that she'd been left-handed. At the end of the night when I dismantled the intricate designs, I found myself having to deconstruct the braids seemingly backwards to me, a right-handed person. Frustration had been my companion many late nights as I freed my hair. A couple of times, I'd left it styled and went to the studio the next day to have hair and makeup untwine my locks, not wanting to bother with it.

My thoughts were rudely interrupted as the passenger door opened. I feared for my life for a moment as a man slid in, but then I realized it was Jordan.

"What are you doing here?" I hissed, glancing over at the church. "Are you out of your mind?"

"Probably, but I brought you coffee." Well, that did make things a little bit better. "Have you seen anyone arrive?"

I shook my head, my mouth watering at the smell of the caramel latte. I took the cardboard cup and sipped greedily. "Are you trying to bribe me to allow you to stay?"

"Maybe," he replied. "Is it working?"

Taking another drink, I nodded. "Yes."

"Jeez, Sam. If I'd brought you a muffin, you'd probably marry me if I asked."

I shot him a glare, but he didn't meet my gaze. Instead, he glanced around the parking lot. "This place is empty," he said. "Someone has come to pay their respects, right?"

"I would hope so," I said. "But I think it's a mistake that you're here. *You are the main suspect in the murder investigation!*"

"No need to remind me of that," he replied,

running a hand through his thick salt and pepper hair. "I'll stay hidden. Since you parked in the shadow of this tree, I didn't even know you were in here until I was almost on top of the car. No one will be able to see me."

I sighed but remained quiet. I had a latte to finish before it went cold.

A few moments later, a car parked directly in front of the church. Katrina exited and walked inside, solo. "Is she married?" I asked. "I can't remember if I ever saw a wedding ring on her."

"Divorced," Jordan said. "She's got a couple kids who live out of state. Are you surprised to see her here?"

"Not really," I replied, shrugging. "Brittney was her employee."

"An employee who stole from her," Jordan pointed out. "I wouldn't think she'd want to say goodbye."

"Well, it's a nice gesture and if she wasn't here, to me she'd look guilty."

Jordan didn't get the chance to answer for another car drove into the parking lot and pulled in a few spots down from Katrina's.

When the man got out, Jordan said, "That's Billy, Brittney's boyfriend."

Tall and lanky with a mess of blond hair, he

wore a navy-blue suit and white shirt. I jammed my coffee into a cup holder and hurried over, hoping to catch him before he entered the church. My Zumba lessons had set every tendon and muscle in my legs on fire, and I felt more like a duck waddling across the parking lot than a human being. Was I being an incredibly insensitive jerk? Yes. But Jordan's freedom was on the line.

"Billy!" I called, trying to walk in as normal a way as possible. He turned as I approached.

"Can I help you?" he asked.

"Yes," I said, stretching my hand. "I wanted to talk to you a minute about Brittney."

A shadow crossed over his blue eyes as he bit his lip. Had I brought him to tears with just the mention of her name? Jeez, I was such a turd.

"What about her?" he asked in a soft voice, then cleared his throat.

"I can see you're upset at her passing," I murmured, feeling awful for ambushing him like I was. I regretted my plan to talk to those arriving at the funeral.

"Very much so. I loved her." Furrowing his brow, he added, "Who are you again? I didn't catch your name."

"Sam Jones," I said. "Sorry about that. I'm

working with a friend who is considering writing a book about the murder. I'm just getting background information."

He shook his head. "I don't want any part of any book about Brittney. I don't want my name mentioned."

"Oh, we wouldn't use your name if you didn't want us to," I replied. "Like I said, we're just looking for background information. Can I ask you a few more questions?"

*Please don't walk away. Please don't walk away.* If I were in his shoes, I would have.

He sighed, glanced at the church, then at his phone. "I've got a couple of minutes before the service begins."

I took that as a yes. "Why did you move after her death?"

"Why wouldn't I?" he asked. "I'd lost the woman I loved more than my own life. Why stick around when it all hurt so bad? I needed to put space between me and what happened."

"Weren't you afraid it would make you look guilty?"

"I don't care," he replied, shrugging. "I told the cops where I was going, gave them my phone number and told them to call me if they needed me for anything. I didn't kill her, so I didn't see that it mattered whether I stayed in town or not."

He'd left days after the murder. How did someone tidy up their life so quickly? When I'd disappeared from my life in Hollywood, I'd literally left with everything on fire. "Did you two rent a place?"

"Yeah, a month-to-month joint. That's why it was so easy for me to walk away. I literally had nothing here to hold me back." He glanced away as tears welled in his eyes and a little guilt tugged at me for putting them there.

"Some say you two had a volatile relationship," I ventured.

"Volatile, passionate… is there much of a difference?"

"Well, yes," I replied. "One is usually a negative experience, the other isn't."

"Passion can be volatile," he said. "Brittney and I were very passionate people. Passionate about each other, about our lives. We loved hard, we fought hard. Our relationship was… I guess the way I'd describe it is as a relationship of extremes."

Okay, this sounded volatile to me, but I wouldn't argue semantics if it kept him talking.

"What about Starlight?" I asked.

"What about her?"

"I understand the two fought quite a bit."

"Definitely. They didn't get along. Brittney said Starlight's boyfriend—his name's Rocky—creeped her out a bit because he was always hitting on her."

Biting my lip, I tried to keep the surprise from my face. Starlight said that Brittney had hit on her boyfriend, not the other way around. Someone was lying, but something stopped me from digging in to find out the truth. Maybe it was all that passionate volatility he mentioned. I didn't want any of it directed at me.

And that gave me pause. Was I afraid of this man? Perhaps a bit, even though he'd done nothing aggressive toward me.

"I don't know who killed her," Billy continued.

"If you had to guess, who do you think it would be?"

"The cops told me that it was one of their deputies. Brittney said one of them sexually harassed her when she worked there."

"Harassed or assaulted?" I asked. There was a big difference between the two.

"*Harassed*," he said. "No one laid a hand on Brittney. Not on my watch."

"Did she give you the name of the deputy?"

He shook his head. "If I ever found out, I'd kill the guy."

Brittney hadn't shared the depth of the allegations she'd launched against Jordan with Billy, which made me question their validity. If Jordan had assaulted her as she claimed, wouldn't she want comfort from her boyfriend? Or had she truly been afraid Billy might have flown off the deep end and try to hurt Jordan?

"Let's say it wasn't the cop who killed Brittney," I ventured. "Who do you think did it?"

With a sigh, he rubbed his forehead with his thumb and stared at the ground for a long time. Finally, he met my gaze. "Honestly, I think if the cop's not guilty, then it was Katrina."

"And why do you think that?"

"She didn't pay Brittney well," Billy said. "To make ends meet, Brittney offered to give some clients private lessons outside the studio."

Finally, something that jived with what I'd been told in the past!

"I'm sure that upset Katrina," I ventured.

"Oh, yeah," Billy replied. "I don't know how she found out, but she did and let Brittney have it."

Arching an eyebrow, I crossed my arms over my chest, goosebumps pricking my skin. If Katrina had actually said that, it would be pretty damning. "Did you tell the sheriff about this?" I asked.

He shook his head. "She never asked me about it and honestly, I just wanted to get the heck out of Dodge." He glanced around the parking lot. "I wasn't even sure if I should come today. I used to love this town, but now... now it just makes me really sad."

Either Billy deserved an Oscar or he hadn't had anything to do with Brittney's death. I couldn't wade through what was the truth while standing in front of him, though. "I'm sorry for your loss," I said.

Another car pulled up behind me and I glanced over my shoulder.

"Speak of one of the devils herself," Billy muttered as Starlight stepped from the passenger side of the vehicle. A man exited the driver's side, and I guessed it was Starlight's boyfriend. Standing at average height and bulky, as if he lifted weights, he eyed Billy warily.

The two approached us and I could feel the testosterone rise and surround us like a heavy fog... or passionate volatility.

"Hi, Billy," Starlight said. "How're you doing?"

"I'm fine," he replied, never taking his gaze off

Rocky. "You got a lot of nerve showing up at Brittney's funeral."

"We're here to pay our respects," Starlight shot back. "Let's go, Rocky."

She grabbed the man's hand and pulled him toward the door while Billy stared until they were inside.

"I can't believe they're here," he muttered. "It's bordering on rude."

"Because she and Starlight fought so much?"

"Yeah, and because Rocky was hitting on her. It all just seems so wrong to me."

There was that point of contention again. Who had been flirting with whom?

I tried to think of any other questions I had for Billy and came up empty-handed. "Thanks for your time," I said as the music started from inside the church. "I appreciate you speaking with me."

"Remember I don't want my name in any book," he said, pointing his finger inches from my face.

Talk about rude... and volatility. "Don't worry. That won't happen."

As I returned to the car and Billy went inside, I couldn't help but wonder if the relationship between Brittney and Billy had become so passionate, he'd killed her.

# CHAPTER 12

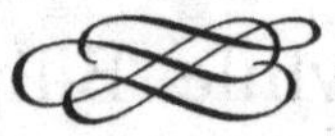

When I returned to the car, Jordan asked, "Find out anything new?"

I shook my head and reached for my latte. "Just more confusion." As I explained the discrepancies in the stories I'd heard, he furrowed his brow.

"I wonder who's lying?" he muttered, staring at the church.

Just as I was about to answer, a sheriff's car pulled in. Jordan swore and sunk down into the seat.

Mallory Richards exited the vehicle and I debated whether to go speak with her or not. I disliked the short, muscular woman, but the more I stuck my nose where it didn't belong, the more certain I became that Jordan hadn't killed anyone. Yes, I still had some doubts, but they were slowly fading.

The sheriff walked into the church.

"What's she doing here?" I asked.

"Just seeing who's attending and who isn't," he replied. "Sometimes it's good to take a look at who cared enough to come."

"If I killed someone, I'd never go to their funeral," I muttered.

"Well, then that may also make you look guilty," Jordan said. "If you kill someone and go to mourn their passing, you either feel awful that you offed them, or you truly miss them."

My thoughts returned to Billy. I had no doubt he loved Brittney. Had he killed her in a rage, and now was back because he felt remorse? He said he'd left because he wanted to get away. Maybe guilt had been the driving force?

I should've asked him if he knew how to braid hair. Something about the braids really bothered me, but I couldn't place why.

But I did have one suspect I could ask who was practically sitting on the floor of my car hiding from the sheriff.

"Did you ever braid Mattie's hair?"

The question caught him off guard and his head snapped up. "Why?" he asked.

"I was just curious. Do you know how to braid?"

He sighed. "Yes. I used to braid Mattie's hair for her."

I nodded, reminding myself that didn't necessarily mean he killed Brittney. Or if he had, he'd been creative in the method. I had been hoping he'd never learned to braid and I could take that to the sheriff and tell her to shove it where the sun don't shine.

As she strolled out of the church, she glanced around, her gaze landing in our direction.

"She sees us," I said. Jordan cursed and tried to make himself smaller. "If I leave now, it will look bad."

"Agreed. Especially if she finds out I'm hiding in here," Jordan replied.

When she stepped off the curb and began walking our way, I jumped out of the car and slammed the door, hurrying to meet her as far away from Jordan as possible. Being caught at the woman's funeral he was accused of killing wouldn't be a good look for him.

"Sheriff!" I called forcing a wave and smile. I

really disliked the woman. "Just the person I wanted to talk to!"

Good grief, my hips and back hurt from Zumba. I didn't know how many more dance classes my body could take.

"What are you doing here?" she asked as we met in the middle of the parking lot.

"I wanted to see who was attending Brittney's memorial," I said. "What are you doing here? Were you friendly with the deceased?"

She shook her head. "I'm investigating the murder. Why do you care who's here?"

The truth lay on the tip of my tongue—I was trying to clear Jordan—but I opted for Gina's lie instead. "My friend is considering writing a book on the murder. She asked me to come and see who was attending the funeral since she's busy and couldn't be here."

Mallory nodded. "Who's writing the book? Why haven't they interviewed me?"

"I really don't know why she hasn't reached out to you," I said. "Should I tell her you're interested in speaking with her?"

"Most definitely. I'm certain we've caught the killer and my insight would be helpful to her."

Or helpful to Mallory's ego, but I'd let that one slide.

"Would that be Jordan?" I asked. "Is he the murderer?"

Mallory nodded. "We're just about done with the investigation. He's as guilty as the day is long."

"Are you sure about that?"

I immediately regretted my question as Mallory's cheeks turned crimson. Because of my dislike of her, I'd never really gotten to know her, but Jordan had shared again and again that she hated being doubted.

"Why in the world would you ask me that?"

I shrugged and replied, "While helping my friend with her book, I've realized there are a lot of other people who wanted Brittney dead. Have you looked into any of them?"

"Like who?" she asked, narrowing her gaze.

"Well, like her boss, for one. Her co-worker, second, and third, her boyfriend. Forth, a woman who claims Brittney stole from her and has a braiding tic."

Mallory shook her head. "None of those people did it. Jordan has the best motive."

"What motive?" I asked. "That he was a target of a fraudulent accusation of sexual assault and the subsequent investigation into those charges?"

As she crossed her arms over her chest, she

also straightened her spine. I should've driven away instead of tangling with her.

"You and Jordan are close, right? I'd heard he was dating you."

"You heard wrong. I don't date."

"Why is that, Ms. Jones? A pretty woman like you… do you really want to spend the rest of your life alone? Why *aren't* you married?"

"I enjoy my own company," I said, noting how she'd flipped the conversation so it was now about me. "What about you? Why aren't you married?"

"You haven't been around here long, but it seems you've become quite the thorn in my side, sticking your nose where it doesn't belong. Where did you say you came from again?"

"California," I said, refusing to be intimidated. "But can we get back to my question? Why won't you investigate anyone else besides Jordan? Do you have it out for him?"

I was pushing too hard, but this woman's smugness and superior attitude made me run my mouth.

"No, I don't have it out for him, but that man has a shady past. He's done this before."

"You mean the incident with his wife and daughter where he was cleared?" I asked.

"You mean where he killed the witness?" Mallory hissed. "Yes."

"I take it you thought he was guilty when you hired him," I said. "If that was the case, then why did you employ him?"

"I was willing to give him a chance when he showed up here because I desperately needed the help. Trying to fill a position of a sheriff's deputy in a small town is difficult. Most want more action."

"And since he's been here, how has his performance been?" I asked. "Any problems?"

She shook her head. "But I obviously made a mistake hiring him."

"Or you're being short-sighted now," I said. "Jordan didn't kill anyone."

"Prove it."

"First, ask yourself how did he get into the dance studio? I understand the murder happened after hours. It's not like he could just walk in."

Her angry gaze never left me, but she didn't answer my question.

"And then take a look at the man you've known in the years he's been here," I said. "Have there been any other examples of poor behavior? Has he ever been written up, or has he done his job with integrity?"

A flicker of doubt crossed her face, but her stubbornness returned quickly. "Ms. Jones, I suggest you stay out of police business and quit telling me how to do my job."

"I'm not telling you how to do your job," I sighed. "I'm asking you to

consider that maybe Jordan is innocent. There are other people who had the motive and opportunity to kill Brittney."

"But there isn't anyone who has gotten away with something like this before." She placed her hands on her gun belt and smiled. "And just as a reminder… if you interfere, you could find yourself behind bars. Good day, Ms. Jones."

She turned and strolled back to her car as if she didn't have a care in the world. I stayed put until she'd driven out of the parking lot, then returned to my vehicle where Jordan was still crouched down in the passenger seat. "She's gone," I muttered as I slammed the door.

"Thank goodness," he said, groaning as he sat up. "My legs are asleep."

"That's the least of your worries, Jordan."

"What did she say?"

"Not much, but she's convinced you're the one who killed Brittney."

"I told you that already, Sam."

With a nod, I pulled out of the parking lot, my heart thundering with dread. Did I tell him that she was looking to arrest him in the near future? But what if I'd somehow convinced her to look at other suspects? I'd worry him for no reason. Maybe she'd just been talking big because of her ego. "Where can I take you?"

"Don't do this," he said. "Don't shut me out."

"I'm not," I snapped. "I just need to think. Where do you want to go?"

"You can drop me right here," he said. I pulled over in front of the grocery store. "Can I call you later?"

"Yes. That's fine." I turned and smiled at him, hoping to convey that everything was going to be okay, when my gut screamed otherwise.

I knew Mallory had Jordan in her sights, but I hadn't realized she wouldn't listen to any reason, even though he'd already explained that was the case. I thought maybe I could make her question her decision, but apparently not.

My conversation with her had only affirmed I needed to find the killer or Jordan was going to prison.

My phone alerted me to a text message and I glanced over at it sitting in the cup holder next to my dead latte. Annabelle. I picked it up and glanced at the screen.

"Oh, gross," I muttered and set the device down on the passenger seat. Why in the world was she sending me a picture of a dead fish?

# CHAPTER 13

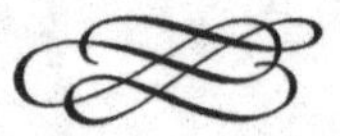

BEFORE DRIVING BACK to the store, I filled up Annabelle's gas tank to say thank you for allowing me to use her car. I still had my eye on a cherry red Ford F150, but had decided to put the money toward the Sage Advice deck instead. Hopefully, by the end of the year, the deck investment would be paying off and I'd be able to walk into the dealership and plunk down a stack of cash for the truck.

Arriving back to the store, I found Annabelle standing at the counter with two men. We didn't get many men in the store and for a second, I thought it may be Doctor Butte and someone else, but when the guy on the left turned around, I realized it was my contractor, Mike. As I approached, I noted Mike's eyes were a little glassy, and I smelled the distinct odor of fish.

"Hey, Sam," he said, pointing to his friend. "This is Richard, the guy who's going to write the environmental report for you."

Richard turned and grinned. In his thirties, bald and a little heavy, his eyes were also glassy. The odor of beer wafted off both of them.

"It's nice to meet you," I said, instead of freaking out that my store now smelled like fish and beer. "I take it you two went fishing?"

Mike nodded. "We did. We finished up about an hour ago and Richard just did the evaluation."

As I smiled, I didn't bother to question if a drunk man should be conducting environmental inspections.

"I'll have it in to City Hall by tomorrow afternoon," Richard said.

"That's much quicker than I anticipated," I gushed, now excited. "Thank you so much!"

"Sure. If there's one thing I hate, it's pettiness, and after what Mike told me about the report and the guy who filed the grievance, Butte's level ten."

I wouldn't argue that, except Butte's pettiness may be a level fifteen to twenty.

"We also brought you a fish," Mike said. "Hope you like trout."

In fact, I detested seafood, but I smiled and thanked them for their generosity. No sense in upsetting the inspector bearing gifts.

We chatted a few more minutes, then the men left. I turned to Annabelle. "Where's that fish?"

"Right here," she said, holding up a brown paper bag. "I was going to put it in your fridge upstairs."

I shook my head. "I don't want it. I hate fish. You go ahead and keep it."

"Okay. I'll still put it upstairs or it's just going to go bad and stink even more."

"Maybe put it in Bonnie's apartment," I called out as she walked through the back room. The last thing I needed was Catnip crying that he couldn't get to the delicacy in the fridge.

Time to get to work, but first, I needed to air out the store. After propping open the back door, I took a moment to envision my new deck and for a second, excitement overrode the building dread within me. I had to concentrate on my business for a bit. Not decks or murderers.

I went over our inventory notes and sat down at the computer to place an order for some herbs we'd need in the near future. One of my goals with the new deck was to grow some of our own that we used on a regular basis. Not only would it cut costs, but it would add to the ambiance of the space. Annabelle had mentioned growing some mint, but I wanted to look beyond that. Lemon balm, arnica, and echinacea were a few that came to mind.

Annabelle hustled down the stairs and took a seat next to me.

"What's up?" I asked.

"I need a favor," she said, her sparkly light blue eyeliner caked on a bit thicker than usual.

"What's that?"

"I want you to go on a car ride with me."

"Where to?"

"I can't tell you."

Sitting back in my chair, I furrowed my brow. "You want me to go somewhere with you but you don't want to tell me where?"

"Exactly."

"What are you up to?" I asked.

"I can't tell you. But will you go with me?"

I sighed and eyed my friend. "Am I going to get in trouble if I do? Because I've got enough trouble on my plate to last me the rest of my life right now."

She shook her head. "Nope. There won't be any trouble."

"When did you want to leave?" I asked,

glancing at the computer screen to check the time. Where in the world had the day gone? Chasing down leads in Brittney's death had eaten up more hours than I'd anticipated.

"After closing is good," Annabelle said, standing. "Thanks, Sam. I appreciate you trusting me."

My answer didn't really reflect a level of trust in Annabelle as she indicated—more curiosity than anything. I did trust her up to a point, but I doubted I would ever fully trust anyone ever again. What was that woman up to?

I finished the ordering, then did a quick sweep of the store, looking for any products out of place. A couple tinctures were not lined up properly, but overall, everything looked great.

Annabelle trotted down the stairs humming Bon Jovi's *You Give Love A Bad Name*. Being with her had reintroduced me to the era I'd long forgotten and I did have to admit, her musical choice grew on me daily and brought back a host of fun memories.

"Did I tell you about the time I met John Bon Jovi at the Viper Room in Los Angeles?" I asked.

She stopped and turned, her mouth a perfect O, her eyes just as wide. "How could you, like, not tell me about that?"

"Sorry," I said, laughing. "Sometimes these

memories just pop into my mind. You were just humming one of his songs, and here we are."

"Well, keep the stories coming," she said. "I love living vicariously through you. Is he as sexy in person as he is on the covers of magazines?"

I nodded. "And that smile truly lights up the room." As I recounted my evening so many decades ago, Annabelle listened intently. For a brief period of time, I forgot about the murder, the suspects, the sheriff and Jordan.

Until he walked in. As I groaned, my stomach flipped and flopped, my stress returning to uncomfortable levels.

"Can I talk to you a minute?" he said. It was then I realized he wore a baseball cap—something I'd never seen him in before—and his sunglasses, along with the ugliest yellow, purple, and blue flannel coat I'd ever seen. I also observed the tag hanging from the armpit, so he'd either just purchased it or he'd never snipped it off.

"What's up?" I asked, now curious about his get up.

He cleared his throat, took off his sunglasses, then glanced at Annabelle. "In private," he murmured. "I'd like to talk to you in private."

"Rude," Annabelle said, tossing her hair over her shoulder. She headed into the back room, returning a moment later with her purse in hand. "I'm going to grab a sandwich at Subs and Smiles. I won't be bringing one back for *you*, though, deputy."

Jordan sighed and pulled off his hat as Annabelle left the building. "Do you think she's really mad at me?" he asked.

I shrugged. "If she is, she'll get over it." My mood continued its downward spiral at an alarming rate. "What's up?"

"Well, I was on my way home from the church when my buddy at the sheriff's office called me," he said.

"And?"

"They were on their way to my house for a search and to arrest me for Brittney's murder."

Goosebumps traveled over my skin as a lump of anxiety fully filled my chest. I should've told him in the church parking lot. "So she's pulling the trigger on arresting you." Obviously, everything I'd said to her earlier in the day had gone in one ear and out the other. It may have even pressed her into speeding up her investigation and subsequent arrest.

"Yep. Instead of heading home, I turned around and went to the second-hand store to grab something that would conceal my identity a little until I could find somewhere to hide."

I took him in from head to toe once again. He'd never been concerned about fashion, but the coat went beyond dreadful. "That jacket is horrid—and something you wouldn't wear. You did well."

"Thanks. I thought it was ugly, too."

"So what are you going to do?" I asked. "Are you really running from the police?"

"Yes, I am." He crossed his arms over his chest. "I'll never make it in jail, especially if they send me out of town. Criminals like to get their revenge on police officers in prison. I've put a few people away who would love nothing more than to shank me."

Of course I didn't want to see him hurt, but it seemed he was running out of time and the net was closing in around him. "You can't hide forever, Jordan."

"Not forever, but hopefully long enough so that you can find the real killer."

I rolled my eyes. No pressure or anything. "Jordan, that could take weeks… months even! That's only if I get lucky and something falls into my lap!"

"You'll figure it out," he said. "You're smart and you've solved murders before. You got this."

A headache formed behind my eyes and I rubbed my forehead with my thumb. "Where are you going?"

"I'm not sure," he replied. "I was hoping I could crash here for a day or two until I figured everything out."

"Here?!" I shrieked. "You want to stay here?"

"I know it's asking a lot, Sam. But my back's against the wall at this point. I've got nowhere to go."

As I stared at him, fury rose within. With him staying here, wouldn't that be considered aiding and abetting a criminal? Could I go to jail for that? How dare he pull me into his mess?

But then I realized that I was already in neck deep. What were another few inches so I could fully drown? "Two days, Jordan," I said. "If the sheriff comes here looking for you and if there's any way I can get into trouble, I'll serve you up to her without a second thought."

"Understandable," he said, smiling. "Thank you. I'll be out of your hair as soon as I can."

I nodded and pointed up the stairs. "Stay hidden in Bonnie's apartment. You better not turn the lights on, either. It's been dark for too long and people will wonder who's in there. It's not going to take Mallory long to show up."

He followed me into the workroom and I pulled my keys out of my purse. I may not like Mallory, but she wasn't stupid. She knew I was poking my nose in Brittney's murder and she was also aware of my friendship with Jordan, even thinking I was dating him. "Here," I said, handing him the keys. "Make yourself scarce."

"Thanks again, Sam," he said, flashing his best George Clooney grin.

Just as I heard the apartment door close upstairs, the front door opened. Annabelle had returned.

"What's going on?" she asked. "What was up with Jordan?"

For a moment, I debated whether I should lie to her but decided against it. She'd eventually hear him moving around upstairs.

"Jordan's going to stay here for a bit," I said. "But you can't tell anyone."

"Okay," she said glancing up the stairs, then lowered her voice. "Are the police looking for him?"

I nodded.

"How long is he going to be hiding out here?"

"I don't know," I replied. "Not long."

"Are you still looking for Brittney's killer?"

"Yes."

"This has a bit of an Anne Frank feeling to it," Annabelle whispered. "He's hiding from Mallory and her Nazis."

A bit overdramatic, but I couldn't disagree.

"Are you still coming with me on my errand?" she asked.

I'd forgotten all about it, and it was the last thing I wanted to do, even though I had no idea where we were going. However, if I wanted her to keep mum about Jordan, then I should play along. "Of course. When do we leave?"

"In about an hour," she said.

"Excellent," I replied, forcing a smile, suddenly exhausted. "Can you tell me what we're going to do?"

She shook her head. "Nope."

Both intrigued and a little worried, I pulled my hair into a ponytail and tried to concentrate on anything but Annabelle's mysterious errand. I had too much going on, too many balls up in the air, which made it impossible for me to focus.

What was she getting me into?

# CHAPTER 14

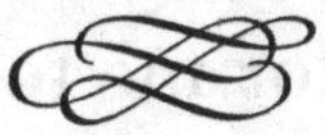

DARKNESS HAD DESCENDED and Annabelle drove slowly in a neighborhood I'd never visited. The large homes were tucked away off the street behind walls of hedges or fences while expensive cars were parked in the driveway or on the street. I still had no idea what we were doing.

"Here it is," she whispered, pulling to a stop and turning out the headlights.

I glanced around. "Here is what?"

She smiled and reached into the back seat, grabbing a paper bag. "You'll see. Stay here."

Before I could question her further, she exited the car and crept down the well-lit street. She stopped at a car and slowly opened the door, then knelt down onto the pavement. I pushed my glasses up my nose and squinted, trying to make out what she was doing. After a moment, it appeared she'd pulled out the interior panel of the door. With her back to me, I couldn't see what she did next, but the low glow of the interior light was strong enough for me to see her putting the panel back in place.

As she gently shut the door and ran back to the car, I shook my head and crossed my arms over my chest. Whose car was this? And what had she done? Was she stealing something?

"What was that all about?" I asked as she slid into the driver's side. She carried the brown bag crunched up in her fist, but nothing else. There hadn't been a theft. Did I smell… fish?

"Let's get out of here, then I'll explain everything."

We pulled away from the curb, Annabelle keeping the headlights off until we were turning onto the main drag, Comfort Road.

"Annabelle, what was that?" I asked again. "What did you do to that car?"

"That was revenge," she said, her face breaking out into a large smile.

Uh oh. I didn't like the sound of that. "Revenge? On who? For what?"

"I've been giving a lot of thought about how to

get back at Butte for submitting that environmental complaint."

I swallowed the bile rising in my throat, unsure if I wanted to know what she'd done. "Was that… were we just at Butte's house?"

She nodded. "Yup. Messed with his car a little bit."

Glancing over my shoulder, I half-expected sheriff's vehicles behind us. Surely, he had outside cameras or some type of security system. If he didn't, then a neighbor would.

"What did you do to the car?"

"Well, you know the fish neither of us wanted?"

I nodded.

"I was going to throw it away, but then I had a great idea. When I put it upstairs, I wrapped it in plastic and set it in the freezer so it didn't stink too bad. Then, back there, I put it in the interior panel of the door. It'll take days before he figures out that he's got a dead fish in there but until then, it'll slowly rot, causing his car to stink!" She threw her head back and laughed. "I wish I could be there to see it all!"

Stunned, I couldn't seem to form words. Part of me wanted to turn around, grab the fish, and apologize to him because there was no way

Annabelle could pull a stunt like that and not get caught. But then again, Butte had been a thorn in my side since the day I moved here, so maybe a little revenge wasn't a bad thing.

"Aren't you worried about being seen?" I asked.

She shook her head. "I've been watching his place for a few days and scoping out his neighbors. There's only one who has a camera, and he's a few houses down. Where we parked, the camera can't catch us."

"You've been watching his house?"

"Yes. Ever since we were, like, told about the environmental concern he filed I've been trying to figure out our revenge." She sighed and smiled. "Payback feels so good."

Sweet Annabelle had a bit of a dark side, which shouldn't have surprised me. She'd also broken into Gina's ex-husband's house and stolen thousands of dollars he'd kept there. Her wanting retribution against Butte seemed like a natural thing, but her daily demeanor didn't mirror this Mr. Hyde persona she pulled out every now and then. I found it amusing, but also a little worrisome. God help me if I was ever caught up on her bad side.

"I think it's great you're helping out Jordan,"

she said, changing the subject. "He didn't kill Brittney. I know it in my heart."

I'd almost forgotten about him. Annabelle may feel that way now, but what would she say if I shared his questionable past?

But then again, the few days of my life prior to me leaving for Heywood had been pretty sketchy as well. Didn't everyone deserve a chance to start over and rebuild their lives? It was what I'd done, and Jordan had as well. The only difference was he didn't know about my dead husband, my life as a Hollywood starlet, or the millions of dollars Gerald had stolen. And I hadn't been accused of killing anyone until I arrived in Heywood.

"Hopefully, Sheriff Mallory won't come sniffing around looking for him," I muttered. "I could get into a lot of trouble. Aiding and abetting, or something like that."

We drove a couple of blocks in silence. Finally, Annabelle said, "Sometimes, you have to do things that may be questionable for people you believe in."

But did I really believe in Jordan? The fact I had him hiding out in my building, for which I could get in big trouble, led me to think so.

"It's crazy," Annabelle continued. "Right now,

you put yourself on the line for him. And who knows? Dating him will probably come next."

As she pulled up in front of Sage Advice, I sighed and shook my head.

"But I know," she said, giggling. "You don't date."

I exited the car and headed inside. Glancing up at the building, I was relieved to see darkness. It didn't look like anyone was around, which was exactly how I wanted it.

After unlocking the door, I slipped inside and then secured it again. I stood at the entrance for a long moment, listening. Nothing *sounded* different, but I knew Jordan was there. The building *felt* different, and I found myself walking quietly through the display tables as if I didn't want to disturb him.

While I crept up through the back workroom and up the stairs, I held my breath. Exhausted, I didn't want to chance running into Jordan. I simply wanted to fall into my bed with Catnip and forget this long day.

My phone sounded loudly in my pocket as I reached the landing, causing me to shriek. The door to Bonnie's apartment swung open, and Jordan stood in the darkness. I couldn't see his face, just his outline, which seemed larger in the dimness than during daylight hours. And a bit menacing.

"Are you okay?" he whispered.

"Yes, I'm fine," I replied, pulling out my phone. "This stupid thing scared me to death."

We stared at each other for a long, uncomfortable moment, then I asked, "How are things going here?"

"Fine. No one's come by."

I tried to imagine sitting in the dark with nothing to do and felt a little bad for him. The guy did need to eat and there wasn't anything in Bonnie's. Against my better judgement, I offered, "Do you want to come in and have a glass of wine? Maybe some food?"

"I thought you'd never ask."

As I walked over to my own apartment, I imagined him flashing me his trademark George Clooney smile. Catnip greeted us and I flipped on the light so I didn't trip over him.

Jordan followed me in, and with a loud groan, took a seat on the couch. "Where did you and Annabelle go?" he asked.

With a snort, I pulled the wine from the refrigerator. "We did something that's probably not legal. Am I talking to a cop or my friend?"

"I'm not a cop anymore… well, at least not for the time being."

After I poured two hefty glasses, I grabbed some cheese and crackers, then joined him on the couch. Catnip jumped up and made himself cozy in Jordan's lap. "So my sins are safe with you? Is that what you're telling me?"

He chuckled and nodded. "Yeah, barring a murder, I don't really care what you did."

I took a long drink, then told him the story. He laughed until tears ran down his cheeks, a reaction I hadn't expected. Perhaps from the stress of his own situation?

I joined in, realizing the silliness of it all. Although, I was certain Doctor Butte wouldn't find it the least bit funny.

"Never expected that from sweet Annabelle," he said, wiping his face. "Thanks for sharing. I needed a good laugh."

We sat in silence for a few moments, each enjoying our wine while he inhaled the cheese and crackers. "Have you heard anything from the sheriff's office?" I asked.

"Yeah, my buddy texted me. He said the sheriff put out an APB out on me. I'm officially wanted for Brittney's murder. They searched my house and impounded my truck."

"I'm sorry," I mumbled, unsure of what else to say. "Did you tell him where you were?"

"No. He didn't ask, and I didn't offer up the information. He did share that they were getting the paperwork to track my phone, so I've turned that off and flushed the sim card."

"What about the crime scene photos I wanted to look at?" I asked. "Can he get you those?"

"Yeah, but I need a phone in order for him to send them. He's going to snap pictures of them and text them to me."

Confused, I furrowed my brow. "But you don't have a phone."

"This is true," Jordan said, sighing. "I was hoping I could ask one last favor from you."

Oh, heck. I'd already put myself on the line for him. "What's that?"

"Can you run to the next town and get a burner phone for me tomorrow?"

After a quick mental recap of my schedule for the next day, I nodded. "I should be able to do that. Why do I need to go to the next town?"

"Because Mallory knows we have a friendship. She'll be watching everyone I know to see if you're doing anything out of the ordinary, like buying a burner."

"Got it. Yes, I can go tomorrow at some point. I'll borrow Annabelle's car again."

"Thanks a lot, Sam. I'll never forget your help, and I have no idea how I'll ever repay you."

"I'll think of something," I said, glancing at my phone. Gina had texted me earlier as I was coming up the stairs and I'd yet to read it.

*Ballet class is at nine in the morning. Are we still going?*

I didn't want to attend, but I also wasn't any closer to finding Brittney's killer. And Jordan was one step closer to going to prison for a crime he didn't commit. The murderer had to be affiliated with Groove and Go Dance—that I knew in my soul.

Ballet class it would be in the morning. I still hadn't recovered from Zumba, so I'd need to take some ibuprofen before going to bed.

*Yes, we're on. See you then.*

"I better get to bed," I said. "Apparently I now have a ballet class in the morning."

Jordan moved Catnip, set down his glass, and stood. "Thanks for everything again, Sam. You're the best."

He grabbed my hand and helped me to my feet. Slowly, he wrapped his arms around me. At first I tensed, but then I placed my head on his chest. My emotions swirled—fear, longing, and sadness. A tear trickled down my cheek as I reveled in the closeness. Somehow, he was projecting how much he cared about me—I could feel it. He placed a small kiss on top of my head and I closed my eyes. I'd never experienced this level of comfort from any man during a hug, even Gerald.

After a moment, I buttoned up my feelings and stepped away. "Goodnight," I said, not meeting his gaze. "I'll bring you something to eat in the morning."

He nodded and turned to leave.

"Jordan? Are you telling me the truth? You didn't kill Brittney, right?"

"I swear to you, Sam. I didn't kill Brittney."

I nodded, still unable to shake the lingering doubt.

When the door softly shut, I sat back down and leaned my head against the cushions, my mind swimming in confusion. Was he trying to break down my defenses so I'd continue to battle for him? Was he manipulating and using me? Or had that embrace really meant something?

"That guy better not be the murderer, Catnip," I whispered. "If he is, I'm going to kill him."

My feline meowed in what I could only assume was agreement.

But if it wasn't Jordan, then who?

I would be so happy if someone would simply confess tomorrow and I could put all this behind me.

# CHAPTER 15

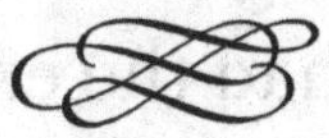

IN THE MORNING, I made Jordan some eggs, a bagel, and a pot of coffee. After exchanging awkward pleasantries, I hurried downstairs to get ready for the day, relieved to be away from him. The hug from the previous night had rattled me to my core, and frankly, I'd become somewhat angry because I felt I didn't know the truth. Was Jordan Brittney's killer? I still wasn't sure, but although all evidence pointed to it, my gut told me he was innocent. Or did I just want him to be?

Despite the fact I didn't want to go to ballet class, I was thankful to be putting some distance between Jordan and me. I felt his presence in the building like a thick fog slowly engulfing and strangling me.

Which was a terrible metaphor because that was exactly how Brittney had been murdered.

I left a note for Annabelle by the cash register, then headed for ballet class. Instead of taking the street, I decided to go via the Riverwalk and check in on Doug. I had the extra time.

As I approached his bridge, I found him sitting on the concrete, his focus on the book in his hands.

"Hey, Doug," I said as I approached.

"Sam! Good morning!" He rose to his feet with ease and grace. Having sat on the concrete pathway many times to talk to him, I always groaned and struggled to stand. I chalked it up to him being a couple years younger than me. "How are you?"

"I'm okay," I said, sighing. "What are you reading?"

"Radical Honesty by Brad Blanton."

"Are you enjoying it?"

He nodded. "It's not your typical self-help book full of warm and fuzzy ideas. It's quite bare bones, no sugar added. Quite bitter, actually."

"So, not a great read?"

"It is," he said. "Sometimes the truth needs to be delivered bluntly in order for people to understand it." He held up the tome. "That's what the author achieves beautifully within the pages."

"Does it share how to discern if someone is telling the truth or not?" I wasn't one to unload my problems on people, but the words tumbled from my mouth before I could stop them.

His smiled faded as his brow furrowed. "Truth is a funny thing. We hope people are honest with us, but most of the time we can never fully know. Heck, it's difficult for us to be honest with ourselves."

"But are there any tips on deciphering if someone is lying?" I pushed.

"Body language usually gives away a lie in most cases. For instance, my cousin always blinks a lot when he's not being truthful. But other people I know… they give nothing away when being deceitful. Well, nothing obvious at least, unlike my cousin."

His kin also happened to be mayor of Heywood, so next time I heard him speak, I'd definitely be studying his eyes and looking for that telltale blink, especially when he spoke about the budget. There were rumblings around town a tax raise may be on the table.

I scoured my brain to pinpoint any of Jordan's

body language that set off my radar and came up empty-handed.

"But overall, truth comes down to our belief in someone," Doug continued. "What's in our hearts? How do we feel about that person? Have they proven themselves untrustworthy to us before?"

I'd hoped for a concrete answer. I didn't want to go into my trust issues or the reason for them.

"I believe Thomas Jefferson said it best when he stated, '"Honesty is the first chapter in the book of wisdom."' Doug's lips curved in a thoughtful smile. "If you think about it, when you don't start with the truth, then everything afterward is wrong."

With a long sigh, I considered his words. Had Jordan been honest with me from the start of our friendship? I believed so. I'd never caught him in any lies. He'd always been an open book when I allowed him to be. But my current dilemma was different because we were talking about murder, and a case that mirrored one from the past.

Suddenly, a thought hit me so hard, I took a step back. Why didn't I look online? There must be some articles on such an explosive police case in Chicago.

"Who are you having a hard time trusting?"

Doug asked. "Maybe I can give you my input if I know them."

I didn't feel comfortable airing Jordan's dirty laundry, especially since it was so stained by past and present circumstances. "Thanks, but it's a very private matter."

Doug nodded. "I understand and admire you for being so discreet. It's a great quality when speaking of honesty."

"Why do you say that?" I asked.

"Because you've most likely given your word to this person that you wouldn't share their problems they trusted you with, and you've proven you won't. It's an admirable trait. William Faulkner said, 'Never be afraid to raise your voice for honesty and truth and compassion against injustice and lying and greed. If people all over the world would do this, it would change the earth.'"

I tried to keep the conversation light because Faulkner was a little too deep for me this early in the morning... Well, most likely, ever. "That's me," I said, a slow heat crawling up my neck. "Keeper of Secrets." And the fighter for justice. But was the person I was protecting actually guilty?

Doug cocked his head to the side. "But I wonder who's keeping Sam's secrets?"

I tried to swallow past the fear rising in my

throat. Did he know what I so desperately didn't want to get out? Was he aware of who I'd been in my past life, and how I'd left it? It was best for me to leave this conversation dead in the water. "I better get going," I said. "Have a great day, Doug!"

Hurrying away before anymore could be said, I felt as if I'd just been skinned alive. Doug was aware of my past. Why else would he say such a thing to me? Unless he *assumed* I had secrets. Didn't everyone? But the way he'd questioned me made me feel there was a deeper meaning.

Or I was suffering from a good case of paranoia. I enjoyed spending time with Doug, but I always felt he was more intelligent than me, and far more perceptive of everything and everyone around him. He saw things in people that I didn't.

I hurried down the Riverwalk until the end, then took the path up to Comfort Road, trying to psych myself up for the ballet class I didn't want to attend.

When I arrived, Gina was already there. She spoke to a few other women I didn't recognize, and I assumed they were other students. I didn't bother to interrupt, but instead watched the group closely. All were dressed in leggings and some type of flowing shirt. It was a bonus that we didn't have to wear tutus for class.

Gina's direct personality was an acquired taste. I found it refreshing after spending my life around the fakers in Hollywood, where I was now convinced I'd had no real friendships. Everyone I'd reached out to after Gerald's death had either ignored me or told me to pound sand. They wouldn't stand by me. But to be fair, Gerald had stolen from a lot of them. None had believed I had nothing to do with his treachery, and they'd left me in the wind to fend for myself.

Gina said something and a few of the women tittered with laughter. However, one who wore unfortunate flesh-toned leggings didn't and excused herself from the group. As she walked over to Katrina, who was speaking to a few other students, she kept glancing over her shoulder toward Gina. She pulled Katrina aside and they had a quick conversation. The studio owner's gaze fell on Gina, then moved to me. Her smiled faded as she pursed her lips.

Gina had obviously said something offensive to the woman, and she'd run off to tattle.

"Uh oh," I muttered as Katrina strode—or floated—toward me, her hands fisted at her sides. I noted the long blonde braid hanging over her right shoulder.

"May I please see you and your friend in my office?" she asked.

I glanced over at Gina. "Sure. Is there a problem?"

"We'll discuss it in private," Katrina said, forcing a smile.

"Where's your office?" I asked.

"Through the arch on the right. Please be prompt in gathering your friend. No dilly-dallying."

I hated when people spoke to me like I was five.

As she turned on her heel and marched toward the arch, I sighed, then went to fetch Gina.

"Katrina wants to see us," I said, smiling at the other women as I gripped Gina's arm.

"Just a sec," Gina replied, meeting my gaze. "I'm in the middle of a story about one of my rescues."

"I don't think that's an option," I muttered, giving her arm a squeeze. "Excuse us." I smiled at Gina's audience then maneuvered her toward Katrina's office.

"What did you say to that woman over there?" I asked, gesturing toward the flesh-toned leggings wearer.

"I told her it looked like she didn't have on any pants," Gina replied.

I stopped and turned to my friend. "You did *what?!*"

"Look at her!" Gina said. "Those leggings make her look like she's running around without any pants on!"

I turned and glanced at the woman. Admittedly, Gina was right, but it would've been best to keep that thought to herself. "Well, you made her mad so she went to tell Katrina, who now wants to see both of us."

Gina rolled her eyes. "And here I thought I was doing her a favor." She glanced at the woman and stuck her tongue out as we passed. "No one likes a tattletale!"

I dragged Gina in through the arch and found another smaller studio that mirrored the other, as well as Katrina's office.

The small space had room for a desk, two chairs and a filing cabinet. Pictures of a younger Katrina dancing hung from the walls. A small silver hook held ballet ribbons, which I assumed were extras for those who needed new ones in their pointe shoes. And it was most likely where the murderer had found the ribbons and weaved them together. How very convenient for Katrina.

"I'm sorry to have to do this, but I would like to request that you two leave the studio and don't return," she said, pulling out a checkbook. "I'll refund you for the thirty-day dance package."

As she picked up a pen, I asked why.

"Because you are asking too many questions about Brittney's death," she said. "You're making my patrons uncomfortable."

Wait. I thought she was going to say we were being banned because Gina was rude.

"Who have we made uncomfortable?" I asked.

"First of all, me," Katrina said. "And poor Gretchen has mentioned you many times. She's almost terrorized. Starlight has also come forward and said your presence and constant questioning make her uneasy." She turned to Gina. "And then you told that woman her leggings made her look like she didn't have on any pants?"

Gina shrugged. "Tell me I'm wrong."

Katrina shook her head and began scribbling across the check. After a few seconds, she ripped it off the checkbook, then wrote out the second. Standing, she handed them across the desk. "Here you go. Refunded in full. Now, please leave the premises."

"This seems a little extreme," Gina muttered, shoving the check in her pocket.

As I took mine, I glanced down at the desktop and noted a stack of flyers promoting the dance contest. "Would you mind if I took one of these?" I asked.

"Go ahead."

"Our friend will want to enter," I said, folding the paper into fourths. "If we come to support her, are you going to kick us out?"

Katrina shook her head. "No, but please don't ask any more questions about Brittney's death. The sheriff says they've caught the murderer. It's bad for my business to have the case constantly brought up. It's time for us to move into the future and unfortunately, that doesn't include Brittney."

Gina pursed her lips and I imagined she was trying to suffocate a smarmy response.

"We'll see you then," I said, turning and heading out the door with Gina behind me.

"You don't know how relieved I am we don't have to take a ballet class," she said.

I couldn't deny I felt the same way, but the door had also just been shut on my only avenue of finding the killer.

# CHAPTER 16

WHEN I RETURNED to the store, Annabelle had arrived dressed in a black Billy Idol t-shirt, a pair of leggings, and high tops. Her hair had been pulled up into a ponytail on top of her head and the crimped locks fell around her head like a waterfall.

"I thought you had ballet class?" she asked, her brow furrowing.

"We did," I replied, hanging my bag on a hook in the workroom. "We were asked to leave."

"Why is that?"

I sighed and placed my hands on my hips. "Katrina said Gina and I made everyone uncomfortable by asking around about Brittney's death."

"That's strange," Annabelle replied. "Why

would asking about a dead woman make anyone uncomfortable, unless they had something to do with her demise?"

"My thoughts exactly," I muttered. "But then Gina also told a woman who was wearing flesh-colored leggings that she looked like she wasn't wearing pants. That may have had something to do with being banned as well."

Annabelle snorted. "Yes, that could definitely be the reason."

"Oh! I have something for you," I said, returning to my bag. I pulled out the dance contest flyer and unfolded it, then handed it to my friend.

"They're going through with it," she whispered, smiling.

"Yes, and I expect you to win."

"This is so exciting!" she squealed. Shaking the paper above her head, she spun around in a quick circle.

Her joy radiated from her and I grinned while she danced. For a second, life seemed so simple. Then I remembered I was harboring a fugitive.

"Have you seen Jordan?" I whispered.

She shook her head. "He's been as quiet as the dead. I wasn't even sure he was still here."

I glanced up at the ceiling. "He should be. He didn't mention he was leaving."

Besides, he'd asked me to get him a phone, and on that phone were going to be the crime scene photos I desperately wanted to see. "Can I borrow your car?"

"Sure." Annabelle pulled her purse out from under the cash register, rummaged around through it, then tossed her keys to me. "Here you go."

"I'll be back shortly," I said. "Thanks a lot."

I didn't bother to inform her of my errand. The less she knew, the better.

As I made my way out of town, my thoughts turned to Katrina's dismissal. Annabelle had been right. Why had she cared we were asking questions about her employee's death, unless she had something to do with it? And how convenient that she kept pointe shoe ribbons in her office. Certainly, she knew how to braid—she'd been wearing one earlier. And I knew she had the strength to kill Brittney, the woman who had pilfered clients and stolen from her.

But did she have the creativity to braid together a bunch of ribbons to strangle Brittney?

Gretchen had that strange braiding tic and she had been so upset with Brittney taking her money then not giving her dance lessons. If she'd been angered enough, she could've strangled

Brittney and she also had access to the studio. Could she plan a murder? She seemed to have the temperament for it.

And then the whole twisted mess with Starlight, her boyfriend, Rocky, and Brittney's boyfriend, Billy had me confused. Starlight and her boyfriend had said Brittney was hitting on him, but Billy had said just the opposite and that Brittney didn't feel safe around Rocky. And then Billy had left town. That made him seem terribly guilty. Even though he'd put on quite the show at the funeral and he seemed sincere, that didn't mean I believed him. But was this all connected to my trust issues or my intuition telling me he was a liar?

"What a tangled web we weave," I said as I pulled into the next town and found a store selling cheap burner phones. I made sure it could receive pictures, paid cash, then hustled to return to Heywood.

Back at the store, I found Annabelle in the workroom hunched over her tinctures listening to The Eurythmics, music I hadn't heard in years. I'd always loved the duo. I'd had the opportunity to meet them back in the day, but I'd come down with the flu and had to skip the concert, something I'd always regretted.

"Hey!" I yelled over Sweet Dreams. Jack and Catnip glanced up from their morning nap, bathed in a sunray coming through the window, then quickly went back to sleep.

Annabelle waved but didn't glance my way. I turned the music down. "Anything from upstairs?" I asked.

"Nope. I swear he's not there. Not even a floorboard has creaked. I always hear you when you're walking around on the second floor. I think he left." She pulled a liquid dropper from a large amber bottle, then slid it into another smaller bottle and squeezed the rubber end of the dropper.

"I'll go check," I said, then turned up the music again before ascending the stairs.

Gently, I tapped on Bonnie's door and wondered when I would stop referring to it as her place.

As I waited for him to answer, I realized Annabelle had been right. Hiding Jordan up here did have an Anne Frank feeling to it.

He opened the door and smiled. I pushed past him and shut my eyes. All the blinds had been closed, and very little light filtered in. What had he been doing all these hours? Staring at the ceiling?

"Hey, Sam," he whispered. "Is everything okay?"

"Fine," I replied, opening my now adjusted eyes. "I got you the phone." Our fingers brushed as I handed him the package and a little jolt of electricity passed through me. Must have been the adrenaline from hiding a fugitive.

As he unwrapped the device and plugged it in, I studied Bonnie's apartment. I should rent it out —a little extra income would be nice. Why was I finding it so hard to move her things and put this space to work for me? She'd left me the building and I knew deep in my heart she'd want me to utilize it to the best of my abilities. But the idea of having a stranger living so close didn't sit well. Maybe I'd become accustomed to living alone and I'd forever be the old spinster in the big building.

*At least I'll have a nice deck in the near future.*

"It's got enough of a charge for me to text my guy at the department," Jordan said, squatting next to the plug where he was powering the phone, his fingers working the keys. "Sent."

"I better get that number just in case I need to reach you," I said.

As he recited it, I put it in my own phone and with a snicker, labeled the number as

George Clooney. Sometimes I cracked myself up.

"I'll go next door and make you a quick lunch," I said, shoving the device in my pocket. "Be right back."

After throwing together a tuna salad sandwich on bread that had expired a week ago, I brought it back to him. I didn't bother to tell him about the out-of-date bread, but hopefully he wouldn't get sick.

We sat on the couch as he ate, neither of us speaking, which was fine with me. I had hoped his friend at the department would get the pictures back to him quickly, but that didn't happen. I considered all the bookkeeping I had waiting for me downstairs, due to my attorney and lawyer, Colin Breckshire, III, in two days. I hated accounting almost as much as I hated Hollywood.

"I need to go," I said, keeping my voice low. "I have work to do. Text me when you get the pictures, or I'll come back up in a few hours to check."

Jordan nodded. "I remember your phone number. And thanks for the sandwich."

"You're welcome."

"I don't want to sound ungrateful, but I think

you better check the expiration date on the bread, though."

I smiled and nodded. "I will. Thanks for the heads up."

Jordan's new phone buzzed and I gently shut the door and returned to the couch while he fetched the device. "It's them," he said. "The pictures."

He sat down next to me and we studied the screen.

I gasped at the photos. Yes, I'd found dead bodies before, but seeing one on the screen still jarred me.

Brittney lay in the middle of the studio, a braided ribbon around her neck, just as Katrina and Jordan had described.

As he flipped through the pictures, I searched for anything that would give away the killer. One of the braided ribbons laid out on a steel table. A close up of Brittney. The fourth picture, which was a wide angle of the whole room, showed something silver lying about fifteen feet from Brittney, but up against the wall. I pointed at it. "What's that?"

Jordan squinted and brought the phone closer. "I don't know," he said. "I don't recall seeing it when I was there."

"Can you make it bigger?" I asked.

He fiddled with the screen and shook his head. "It's still blurry."

"Can you ask your buddy to enhance that?"

"Yeah, I can," he replied, typing on the phone. "No promises on when he'll get back to me, though."

I sat against the cushions and sighed. "Did he say if they're still looking for you?"

"They're checking some of my old haunts. He told me they went to On The River, but Sally wasn't very helpful and didn't recall the last time she saw me."

"My guess is she lied," I said. "It was just a couple of days ago."

"I think you're right. But they're closing in, so I'm thinking I better get moving."

"Where will you go? And what will you do?"

He shrugged. "Maybe I'll just head for the woods."

"Without a tent or anything?" I asked. "With just the clothes on your back?"

"I'm not sure what else to do."

"They'll find you in a second with that ugly jacket," I muttered.

With a chuckle, he shook his head. "I'll get out of your hair tonight. Maybe I can swing by my house and get my camping gear, then head out."

"Won't that be risky?" I asked.

"Yeah, but I don't want you to get in trouble. You've done so much for me already. I'm willing to take that risk. I never unpacked from the last time I went out, so I've got the tent and backpack ready to go. I just need to get in and grab it, then leave."

I tried to imagine being out in the forest, alone, with my tent and a backpack. I wouldn't last more than a day, but Jordan obviously had experience with such adventures, so hopefully he'd be okay. And maybe, if I could figure out who killed Brittney, he wouldn't have to run away. I picked up the phone again and glanced through the pictures, then remembered my book-keeping. Setting down the device, I said, "We'll get it figured out, but for now, I need to get back to work."

With a wave, I exited the apartment and walked downstairs. Annabelle had turned off the music and was speaking to someone in the front of the store. I stopped and listened for a second before making my presence known.

Recognizing the voice, I quickly pulled out my phone and pulled up George Clooney.

*Mallory's here!* I typed.

No reply, but Annabelle came into the back room.

"She wants to talk to you," she hissed, pointing to the front room.

"About Jordan?"

"Yes!"

Crud.

# CHAPTER 17

Taking a deep breath, I smiled and walked into the front room finding not only the sheriff, but another deputy. "Hi, Sheriff," I said. "What can I do for you?"

"Sam! Glad you could finally come down and find the time to speak to me. I was wondering if you've seen Jordan."

"Why? What's going on?"

"Well, I told you we were going to arrest him, remember? It's time. We've built our case and he's going down for Brittney's murder."

I rubbed my sweaty palms on my leggings and tried to calm my flippity-floppity stomach. I didn't want to throw up and give away my nervousness.

"So, have you seen him?" Mallory asked.

"Not recently," I said, mentally redefining 'recently' to only include the past thirty seconds.

The sheriff narrowed her gaze. "I do believe he may be here."

Heat rose in my neck, but I refused to be intimidated by the woman. "Please go look for him somewhere else, Mallory."

I glanced over at her co-worker who stared daggers at me, then shook his head ever so slightly. Was he trying to convey a message to me? Was this the guy on the inside sending Jordan crime scene photos?

"I'd like to take a look around," Mallory said.

"That won't be possible," I stated.

"Why is that?" Mallory asked, placing her hands on her gun belt. Was she trying to frighten me? "Do you have something to hide?"

I crossed my arms over my chest. "No. I just believe in laws, and I don't want you poking around my home and store without a warrant."

"Ah, I see. You want to make this difficult."

"Not really," I replied, shrugging. "Just legal."

I had no training in law or lawyerly matters, but I'd watched enough cop shows that I knew she needed a warrant to look for Jordan. "I don't know why you think he's here, anyway," I said.

"Word on the street is that you two are dating," Mallory shot back.

Stupid gossip vine. "Well, the word on the street is wrong," I said. "I don't date."

"She's not lying about that," Annabelle said, stepping next to me from the back room. "She's going to be an old lady cat spinster."

I threw her a glare.

"Not that it's a bad thing," Annabelle amended. "There are plenty of perfectly happy, content older women who like their cat better than any human."

For some reason, I thought of Gina and her dogs. Annabelle had described her perfectly. And overall, I did appreciate the human species. My problem was that I trusted none of them.

My phone buzzed in my pocket, but I didn't dare take it out. Instinctively, I knew it was Jordan.

Mallory reached into her jacket and smiled. "Well, today is your lucky day, Sam Jones. It just so happens I have a warrant to search your building right here."

Dread sunk into my stomach like a sack of rocks. What the heck did I do now? I wouldn't allow her to see me worry or flinch, though. I had no idea what would happen when she walked up my stairs and found Jordan. Would I go to jail as well for hiding a fugitive? Most likely.

With a sigh, I pulled out my phone, squared my shoulders, and pushed my glasses up my nose. Then, I gave her my best Cassie glare and slid into character with ease, including the haughty voice. "Before you do anything, I'd appreciate it if you'd allow me a quick conversation with my lawyer." I added a smarmy smile for good measure. "I'm sure the people who spread the word on the street would welcome the knowledge that our sheriff was a kind, decent human being."

Just saying the words left a bad taste in my mouth. Mallory was a lot of things, and none of them were kind and decent.

Her gaze flickered as she weighed my words. Elections were coming. She needed all the good publicity she could get, and the gossip vine would be the best way to spread the news of her compassion. "Sure, but hurry up," she grumbled. "We've got a murderer on the loose."

I pulled out my phone and glanced at the screen. As I'd predicted, a text from George Clooney—I mean, Jordan—had come in. Ignoring it, I dialed Colin Breckshire III, and stepped into the workroom. It didn't offer me a lot of privacy, but it was better than nothing.

"Hello, Sam," he greeted me. "How is your day going?"

"The sheriff's here with a warrant to search my property!" I hissed, glancing at the doorway to make sure no one was eavesdropping.

"Oh, my. What have you gotten yourself into now?" I imagined him sitting behind his big desk, straightening his bow tie while furrowing his brow.

"They think I'm harboring a fugitive," I whispered.

"Are you?"

Well, heck. "I have client-attorney privilege, right?"

"Of course. Not only that, you have my friendship, and I don't gossip or rat out my friends."

I felt a little better sharing my dilemma. "I'm sort of harboring a fugitive. I don't think he did what they're accusing him of, though." At least, I was sort of sure he didn't kill anyone. "Does that help?"

"I'm afraid not, Sam," he said, sighing. "Guilt or innocence is not for you to decide."

"What do I do?" I grumbled, squeezing my eyes shut as I pinched the bridge of my nose. A stress headache began to form behind my eyes, which was one of the last things I needed. "If they catch him here, am I going to be in trouble?"

"That depends on a number of different factors," he said. "I would suggest you allow the search to happen, and don't say another word."

"Can you stop them?"

"I'm afraid the answer is no, especially with a warrant. A judge has deemed there's enough evidence to issue it. But I'm at your service, Sam."

"Are you coming here?"

"Yes, I'm on my way out the door. I'm not a criminal defense attorney, but I'll represent you for now and get you one if it becomes necessary."

My shoulders sagged and I sighed in relief. "Should I ask them to wait until you get here?"

"No. Just remain silent, Sam. Say nothing. If they question you any further, simply tell them your lawyer is on his way and they may speak to me when I arrive. Allow them to complete their search."

"Okay. Please hurry, Colin."

"See you shortly."

I hung up and shut my eyes as tears welled, even though I felt slightly better about my situation. Jordan—I'd failed him. But I had to get myself together and face Mallory again. She wouldn't see how upset her presence had made me.

As I swiped my cheeks with my fingers, a hand landed on my shoulder. With a gasp I spun around to find Jordan behind me. I hadn't heard him come down the stairs, and I didn't know whether to be impressed or frightened. Those stairs moaned and groaned with each step, so either he'd somehow learned to move through a space without making a sound, or he was a warlock, vampire, or some other supernatural creature I thought didn't exist and had floated down to the first floor. Or, I was going deaf. I'd prefer him to be a supernatural creature.

"I'm turning myself in right now," he whispered, keeping his gaze focused on the doorway leading to the front of the store where Mallory waited. "I can't have you in trouble."

"Just go out the back door!" I pointed over his shoulder. "Run!"

"To where?"

"Take the path down to the Riverwalk, Jordan. Head out to the forest! Follow your original plan!"

He shook his head. "If she finds out I was here, she's going to make your life miserable. I'm not going allow her to do that to you."

"Ms. Jones?" Mallory yelled. "Let's go. I don't have all day."

"You still have time to get out of here, but that time is ticking by quickly," I hissed, pointing to the door once again.

"No. It's over."

"But it's not, Jordan! I can figure this out! I can find out who really killed Brittney!"

And I realized that finally, I did fully believe in his innocence. No lingering doubts remained.

"I know you will," he said, placing his hands on my shoulders. "I have faith in you. But for now, I'm cornered, and I'm not going to make your life any more difficult."

"Ms. Jones!" Mallory yelled again.

"The phone is upstairs," he whispered, "Under the couch cushion. My guy at the station said he'd blow up that silver thing you found in that picture earlier. I told him I was turning myself in, but you can keep texting him with any questions you have, okay?"

"He's still going to help?"

"Yes. He thinks I'm being railroaded as well."

"What's his name?" I asked.

"Don't worry about that now," Jordan replied. "Just know he's on our side."

"Sam! Time's up!" Mallory boomed, irritation dripping in her voice. I stepped away from Jordan as I heard her boots coming closer. Jordan took a few long strides and met her at the doorway.

Her eyes widened as she glanced up at him and a slow smile spread across her face. "Well, well, well. Look who we have here."

Jordan raised his hands to his shoulders.

"Turn around, Jordan," Mallory ordered. "You're under arrest for the murder of Brittney Fitch."

He did as instructed while I stared at the sheriff, imagining myself flying through the air and landing a perfect roundhouse kick to her face. Of course, I'd never follow through and attempt such a move because I'd most likely break every bone in my body and pull my groin. But I did appreciate the drama of my vision and the idea of my sneaker smashing her nose.

"I knew he was here," Mallory said, her grin indicating she was quite pleased with herself.

"I don't know what you're talking about," Jordan muttered. "I just walked through the back door, up from the Riverwalk. If I'd known the police had arrived, I would never have stopped by."

"You're telling me Sam has nothing to do with

you being in this building?" Mallory asked, the sound of the cuffs clicking locked.

"That's exactly what I'm saying," Jordan grumbled.

I stared at the two, trying to think of anything to say to stop the madness of Jordan being hauled off to jail. Instead, I had fits and starts and nothing coming out of my mouth made any sense.

"Let's go, Mr. Branson," the sheriff said.

Her deputy glanced at me and nodded. Again, I felt he was trying to send me some sort of signal.

As she led Jordan out the front door, I crossed my arms over my chest, my fury brewing. Mallory opened the police cruiser door and Jordan slid in. When she slammed it, I jumped a little. The gesture seemed so final. What if that was the last time I saw Jordan? What if she sent him out of town to jail to await trial, and he was killed by someone he'd put away, as he'd anticipated he would be?

The sheriff pulled away from the curb just as Colin arrived. He hurried from his car and came inside.

"I'm too late," he said, removing his fedora and

glancing over his shoulder at the departing vehicle.

"We all are, Colin," I sighed as tears streaked my cheeks. "We're all too late."

# CHAPTER 18

SHORTLY AFTER MY LAWYER LEFT, I ran upstairs to fetch the phone Jordan had hidden with Annabelle, Catnip, and Jack on my heels.

"What are you doing?" Annabelle asked as we reached the landing.

Through my tears, I explained that someone in the sheriff's department was texting information about the case to the burner phone I'd bought for Jordan and I needed to keep it with me.

"That's sneaky," she said as I pulled the couch cushions off in Bonnie's apartment. The device lay just where Jordan had said it would be. After stuffing it in my pocket, Annabelle helped me right the furniture while Jack sniffed around and

Catnip sat at the door, unwilling to enter the apartment.

"What are you going to do now?" Annabelle asked.

"I don't know," I sighed, plopping down onto the couch, swiping at the stupid tears again. I hated crying. I'd shed enough tears in the days before I left Hollywood to last me a lifetime. "I honestly don't know."

"Well, the way I see it, you have two choices," she replied, sitting down next to me and holding up two fingers. "First, you can sit here and moan and cry about Jordan, or second, you can get out there and prove his innocence."

"I've been trying to do exactly that," I muttered. "And I've failed miserably."

"Yes, you have. But you just haven't figured it out yet. This defeat business written on your face isn't a good look on you."

"What does that mean?" I asked.

"You look like a beaten puppy," she said, shrugging. "I like the strong, take-charge Sam, not this sniveling, little—"

I held up my hand to stop her from continuing. "Okay, fine, I get it, Annabelle. No need for name calling."

"My grandpa always said to pull yourself up by your bootstraps and get 'er done."

"I don't even know where my bootstraps are."

"Now that you say that, I don't, either," she said, staring at my sneakers. "But the moral of the story is still the same. You can't give up on Jordan. If you think he's innocent, get up and go find out who killed Brittney. That's what Cassie would do."

I nodded and tried to find the energy to rise from the couch, but it simply wouldn't come. Catnip stared expectantly at me from the door, his tail swishing back and forth as if he waited for something. Had I fed him today?

Pretty sure I hadn't. I stood and headed for my own apartment. If anything could get me moving, it was my cat. I didn't want him angry at me.

"I'll be downstairs!" Annabelle yelled while I poured food into Catnip's bowl. As he devoured it, I apologized for my oversight and promised him I wouldn't let it happen again. Afterward, I left my apartment door open in case he decided to roam the store.

Annabelle was right. Instead of feeling like a failure for Jordan being booked, it should inspire me to work harder to find the killer.

It had to be someone at Groove and Go

Dance. Brittney didn't seem to have much of a life outside of it. Billy hadn't mentioned any hobbies, and neither had Jordan. Not that he'd really known her, but he was also convinced the killer was associated with the studio.

I needed to clear my head. "I'm going for a walk," I said when I found Annabelle in the store. "I won't be gone long."

"That's fine. I'll just be here practicing my moves so I can beat the pants off everyone else in the dance competition tomorrow."

Was it that soon? I'd grabbed the flyer but hadn't studied it very hard.

She moonwalked across the floor with such ease, I couldn't help but be impressed. "You're coming to cheer me on, right, Sam?"

Initially, I wanted to say no because I had too much going on. I wouldn't enjoy it with Jordan sitting in jail. However, Katrina had granted me access to the studio for the contest to support Annabelle. It was my only way in. "I wouldn't miss it for the world," I said.

"Wait until you see what I'm going to do," she said. "I've got backup dancers and everything. It's going to be amazing."

I wasn't sure where she'd found the time to recruit them, but my curiosity on what she had planned grew. I loved that aspect of Annabelle—predictable was not a word to describe her. The only thing I could count on was her dedication to the eighties.

"See you in a bit," I said, leaving the building.

As I strolled down the street, I tried to open my mind, to think things through without bias—just cold, hard facts.

Why did people kill? Love, money, revenge. And everyone involved had some bone to pick with Brittney that fell under one or more of those umbrellas.

Billy, Brittney's boyfriend? Love. He'd stated more than once Starlight's boyfriend, Rocky, had been hitting on her. But what if that hadn't been the case? What if it had been the other way around, and Billy had flown into a fit of rage and killed his girlfriend?

Katrina. Money. Brittney had been stealing from her by pilfering her clients.

Gretchen—also money. And a strange braiding tic. She was furious with Brittney and Katrina for not getting what she paid for.

Starlight's motive equaled love and revenge. If Brittney had been hitting on her boyfriend, Rocky, Starlight would've been furious and want to retaliate. Besides, it seemed those two were like oil and water. Even taking Rocky out of the equation, they were always fighting.

Every person I'd spoken to had a motive that made perfect sense to me. But who had taken that motive and metaphorically wrapped it around Brittney's neck, choking the life out of her?

As I approached On The River, Rocky walked out the door. Stopping in my tracks, I stared at him for a moment and realized he was the one person in this mess that I hadn't yet spoken to. Some super sleuth I was. He'd been at the funeral, but he hadn't said a word.

No better time than the present to ask a man if he'd been flirting with someone besides his girlfriend.

"Rocky!" I called out as I jogged down the sidewalk, my legs and hips still protesting from my Zumba class.

He turned as I made it to the parking lot and slowed.

"Hi!" I said, approaching him with a smile. "My name's Sam. We met briefly at Brittney's funeral."

"Right," he said. "What can I do for you?"

"Well, I was wondering about your relation-ship with Brittney," I said. "I've heard conflicting stories and I wanted to hear your side of it."

His blue gaze jumped around the parking lot. "I really don't have anything to say about it. She's dead."

"Rocky, did she cause problems between you and Starlight? I heard that she flirted with you, but then someone also mentioned that you were the one who instigated it."

"What does it matter?" he asked, not meeting my gaze. A vein in his neck popped as his hands fisted at his sides. My questioning had hit a nerve. "She's dead and they have the guy who did it in custody. That cop killed her because he raped her and they were investigating it. He didn't want to go down for that, so he got rid of the witness."

What a neat, tidy story. It was so easy to believe, especially if one was also aware of Jordan's past and the mess he'd left in Chicago.

"What if I told you the sheriff is an idiot and she's got the wrong guy behind bars?"

He shook his head and stared at the pavement. Why did I feel Rocky was hiding something from me?

"What if that was you in jail for something you didn't do?" I asked. "Wouldn't you want the truth to come out? You'd want the real killer caught, Rocky. Any sane person would."

Hopefully, he felt the same way and I

hadn't just insulted him by insinuating he was insane for not wanting the same outcome as me.

After a long moment of silence, he spoke. "Yeah, I'd want the killer caught."

"What aren't you telling me?" I asked.

"I have to go," he said, turning away.

"Rocky!" I grabbed his arm. "I feel like you're hiding something from me. What is it?"

He yanked his wrist out of my grasp and faced me. "You want to know who flirted with who? Fine. Both of us were responsible." As he ran a hand through his hair, tears welled in his eyes. "I loved that girl, okay? I loved Brittney, and I was about to break up with Starlight so I could be with her."

Well, color me surprised. I placed my hand on the hood of the car next to me to steady myself, hoping I didn't set off an alarm. I never saw this twist coming.

"D-did Brittney feel the same about you?" I asked.

"She said she did," he sniffed as his shoulders slumped. Jordan had once said real grief had an element that was impossible to imitate. Rocky's sorrow engulfed me like a tangible force. He wasn't faking any of it.

"What about Billy?" I asked. "Did he know about your relationship?"

"I have no idea. Brittney said she was going to tell him, but even though she wouldn't admit it, she was afraid of him."

I stared at him for a moment, trying to put the pieces together. "Do you think Billy killed Brittney? That maybe she did tell him about your relationship?"

"And he decided that if he couldn't have her, no one could?" Rocky said.

"Yes, exactly."

He shook his head. "I don't think Billy had anything to do with it."

"Why not?"

"Because the night Brittney was killed, I saw him down at Hold Your Horses."

The local bar.

"He could've slipped away for a bit to strangle her," I said. "You weren't keeping your eyes on him every second, right?"

"Actually, I was. Brittney and I were texting and she was asking what he was doing every five minutes. She wanted to know when he was headed home and how much he'd had to drink. I also didn't want him coming over to me and finding out I was texting his girlfriend, so I kept an eye on him."

"So you don't think Billy killed her? There's just no way for him to have done so?"

Rocky shook his head. "Not that I can see. We were both at the bar really late, and then he went home."

"What about then?" I asked. "He could've gone to the studio and killed her at that time."

But what had Brittney been doing at the studio so late at night?

"He was out of his mind drunk," Rocky replied. "They literally tossed him into the back of a friend's car and he took Billy home. I told Brittney about it and she said she'd go sleep at the studio so she wouldn't have to deal with him. There was no way he could've sobered up enough to kill her. He didn't even know where she was."

"So you're pretty certain Billy didn't kill her, and you say that you loved her. Who do you think killed her then, if not Billy or you? Katrina?"

He shook his head. "I think Starlight did it," he said. "She suspected something was going on between me and Brittney. I'd caught her more than once going through my phone and she questioned me relentlessly about where I was."

"You're blaming your current girlfriend for

this murder?" I asked, honestly surprised by this turn of events.

"Starlight can be mean," he replied. "And she had a jealous streak. I'd seen her say some horrible things to women just because they spoke to me while we were out and about. She's possessive."

"And you're still with her? If she's so awful, why haven't you broken up with her?"

"Honestly, I'm afraid to," he said. "If she killed Brittney, then what's to stop her from doing the same to me?"

# CHAPTER 19

THAT NIGHT, I scrolled through the pictures on Jordan's burner phone while sitting on my couch enjoying my second glass of wine, Catnip curled at my side. The secret deputy at the sheriff's office had sent over a blown-up picture of the silver thing I'd seen in the murder photos. Turned out it was a barrette, one I felt I'd seen before. It could've been at the grocery store, or possibly on someone at the dance studio, or maybe a magazine. Heck, for all I knew, Annabelle had one just like it, or one of our regular customers wore it a lot. No matter how hard I tried, I simply couldn't place it.

I glanced through the text messages from the mysterious deputy and Jordan.

A few moments before Mallory had stormed in, Jordan had received a text. He must have answered right after I left him.

*Are you at Sage Advice? If yes, we're coming for you.*

*Turning myself in.*

*Why not run for it?*

*Can't do it. I've got to think about Sam. If I run and Mallory finds out I've been here, she's going to crucify Sam. Won't do that to her.*

He'd stayed because he was afraid of what Mallory would do if she discovered I'd been harboring a fugitive. Of course, he'd told me as much, but seeing it in writing only solidified it. The fact it gave me the warm and fuzzies irritated me because it wasn't the emotion I wanted when I thought about Jordan. But what was a girl to do? He'd proven chivalry was alive and well.

With a long sigh, I studied the rest of the photos, taking my time with each one. The braided ribbons held my attention for a long time. Knotted at one end, the strands had been neatly woven together, then tied at the other. But something was off with them and I couldn't place what it was. I moved my fingers across the screen, making it bigger, and for a long moment I forgot it was a murder weapon until I noticed a hair stuck in it. I assumed it was Brittney's. Had it been tangled in the braid while she died?

"Oh, yuck, Catnip," I muttered, then flipped back to the crime scene. Had Starlight killed Brittney as Rocky had thought? Or had he truly done it and now felt desperate, throwing his girlfriend under the proverbial bus? But why? Maybe he guessed the police would never assume she had the strength? He had said he wanted the real killer caught if Jordan hadn't been the murderer. Perhaps the caveat to that was: as long as it wasn't he who was arrested.

I studied the braid again. What about it was bothering me?

After setting down the phone, I used the restroom. I stared at myself in the mirror and ran a hand over my curls, as well as my face. The Botox and fillers had to be completely dissolved by now. Little lines had appeared at the corners of my eyes, as well as the "elevens" between my eyebrows. Pressing my fingers under my chin, I noted my jaw seemed a little slack. I did have to admit, my skin looked great, though. Annabelle's skincare line for mature women worked wonders.

Catnip came to join me and sat down on the toilet tank.

"I have no idea how old you are, but at least you don't get wrinkles," I said. "You remain cute until the bitter end."

He meowed in agreement. Well, at least I thought so.

I took a chunk of my curls and pulled them apart into three separate pieces. Slowly, I placed one chunk over the other. Every now and then, one curl would spring loose and I'd have to start over. After a while, I had three braids in my hair. Considering each one carefully, I sighed. What about that braid in the picture bothered me so much? The answer wasn't to be found in my own hair. Maybe if I braided someone else's and compared it to the photo?

Hurrying back into the living room with Catnip at my heels, I grabbed my phone from the coffee table and texted Annabelle.

*Do you need help getting ready for the dance contest tomorrow?*

. . .

THE CONVERSATION BUBBLE appeared and I waited for an answer.

*I DON'T THINK SO.*

CRUD. I wanted to braid her hair.

*CAN I play with your hair for a bit before you get ready?*

*Why?*

*It's a long story. I can explain tomorrow.*

*I guess so. I'll come pick you up and we'll go to the studio together. That's where everyone is getting dressed.*

HUH. I had no idea. *Sounds great. Thanks.*

As I finished my wine, I sat on the couch and stared at the ceiling, wondering how Jordan was doing. Maybe I could go visit him tomorrow if Mallory allowed it… or hadn't shipped him out of town to some other holding cell. At least if he remained in Heywood, he'd be safe from criminals he'd put away and he had the mysterious deputy looking out for him.

With my wine gone and exhaustion railing through me, I turned to my cat. "I better get to bed, Catnip," I said. "I can't catch a killer without any sleep."

THE NEXT MORNING, Annabelle came by as we'd agreed. I made sure I had my phone, as well as Jordan's burner, tucked safely away in my bag.

"Good morning!" she sang as I slid into the passenger side and noticed she wore her hair down, free of the usual sprays and gels, which was a good thing for me. I'd be able to weave the soft strands together without fighting the styling products she normally overused.

"'Morning," I said.

"What a beautiful day to win a dance contest!"

I smiled, appreciating her positive thinking and confidence.

"Why did you want to help me get ready?" she asked as she pulled away from the curb and into the light traffic of Comfort Road.

I explained that I really didn't have a reason and that I wanted to play with her hair. "There's something about the braid that killed Brittney that's driving me crazy."

She furrowed her brow. "That's weird, Sam. I mean, it's a braid."

"I know," I sighed. "Maybe it's just my middle-aged brain short-circuiting, but I feel like I'm going nuts trying to figure it out."

"Well, you can braid my hair for a bit, but I'll need time to get ready. Oh! Maybe we can incorporate the braids?"

"Your famous Boy George look?" I teased.

"Yes! That's perfect. I was planning to go with something different, but Boy George works. I even have ribbons to include in the style!" She hitched her thumb over her shoulder, and I turned to the backseat to find a large black duffel bag. It looked like she was going on a trip, not to a dance contest.

"What's in there?" I asked.

"Makeup, hair products, a curling iron, and a couple of different outfits for me to try on, as well as some props for my backup dancers."

I wanted to question her further but decided to be surprised instead.

As we drove, I stared out the passenger window, the town slowly going by. Cup of Go. Subs and Smiles. On The River. When we passed Tinkering on Trucks, I grabbed Annabelle's arm. "Stop!" I shouted. "Go back!"

"What! What!"

"Turn around!" I yelled. "Park over there! Across the street!"

"What in the world is going on?"

"Just do it!"

As she made a U-turn and pulled into the parking lot across from Tinkering on Trucks, she said, "You could've caused me to get into an accident, Sam! You scared me to death!"

"I'm sorry," I said, then pointed out the windshield. "But look."

She followed my finger to the auto shop where Doctor Butte stood with his car door open gesturing frantically while he spoke to Harry, the owner.

Annabelle gasped, placing her hand over her mouth. "Oh, my gosh! I was just thinking about Butte yesterday and wondering how his car was smelling!"

"By the look on his face, the odor must be pretty bad."

Butte pointed inside and threw his hands up into the air again while Harry scratched his head.

"I kind of feel bad for Harry," I muttered. "He shouldn't have to deal with this."

"You're right," Annabelle said. "I never imagined he'd go to Harry, but I should've seen that coming. I mean, if something's wrong with your car and you live in Heywood, you go see Harry."

As the mechanic got down on his knees and glanced under the seat, Butte looked our way and Annabelle and I both slid down.

"Do you think he can see us?" I whispered.

"The sun is shining our way, so hopefully there's a bad glare on the windshield."

I peeked above the dashboard again, but Butte was focusing on Harry once again. "I think you're right," I said, sitting upright. "We weren't spotted."

We sat in silence as Harry checked the inside of the car, then moved to the trunk. He shook his head, obviously unsure of where the odor originated.

Butte waved his hands in the air once more, his face turning the shade of cherries.

Harry rubbed his face and nodded, then opened the hood, bent over and checked out the engine.

"I wish we could hear what they were saying," Annabelle said. "Butte's most likely being a jerk to Harry—that we can count on."

"I'm enjoying this way too much," I snickered, crossing my arms over my chest.

"I am too, but we do need to get going."

"Wait just a minute," I begged. "Maybe Harry will start taking apart the car and we'll see Butte's face when he finds the fish."

After a few moments, Harry went inside and returned with a screwdriver.

"He's doing it!" Annabelle squealed. "He's going take it apart!"

Minutes passed as Harry did something inside the vehicle all the while Butte was talking… or possibly yelling. It was hard to tell from a distance. Then Harry got down on his knees and popped the inside of the car door off and jumped away, covering his face when the dead fish flopped to the ground.

Butte stared at the offending trout for a long time while Annabelle and I giggled so hard, tears rolled down our faces. She high-fived me numerous times while Butte began to scream, even going so far as to kick his own tires.

"Isn't revenge sweet?" she asked.

I nodded and tried to catch my breath. "It is. I can't remember the last time I laughed this hard."

"As much as I'd like to continue to watch this, I have a dance contest to win."

"Let's go," I said, sighing. "I'm so glad we witnessed Butte get his."

As she pulled out of the parking lot, my phone buzzed in my purse. I retrieved it, then tapped the screen. My contractor, Mike, had sent a message.

*WE'RE good to go on the deck. Planning to start next week.*

I SMILED AGAIN, very pleased with how the day was shaping up. Now if only I could find Brittney's killer and get Jordan out of jail.

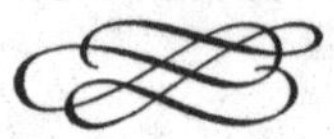

# CHAPTER 20

GROOVE AND GO Dance was buzzing with the excitement of an Emmy awards day. Little girls and a few boys ran around in their costumes ranging from a simple tutu to sparkling body-suits, with their parents chasing them down for a hairdo fix or costume adjustment. Women and a couple of men of all ages took deep breaths in corners. I guessed they were trying to calm their nerves.

The front studio held rows of chairs facing a makeshift stage. One of the back areas had been converted to a dressing room / makeup room. Small white tables with mirrors attached and chairs had been brought in and lined the walls. Each held a place card with two names. Once we found Annabelle's area, I realized she would be sharing with someone named Cayenne.

"Who names their kid after a pepper?" I whispered as we set down Annabelle's gear and she studied herself in the mirror.

"Be nice," Annabelle said. "She's one of my backup dancers."

"How old is she?"

"About twelve, I think," Annabelle said, sitting down in front of the mirror. "Nice girl. She formed my whole posse. Now what do you want to do with my hair?"

I went to her bag and pulled out a brush and a couple of plastic bands. "Right now, I just want to do a couple of quick braids, take pictures of them, then we can work on your hair for the contest."

"Okay, but hurry, Sam. I also have to get dressed and warm up, then make sure my backup dancers are ready to go."

"Yes, ma'am," I replied, running the brush through her hair. "It'll only take a minute or two."

As I sectioned her hair, I concentrated on every move I made. After ten minutes, Annabelle's hair sat in three braids—one on each side of her head and one down the back. And I still didn't have an answer on why the picture of the murder weapon bothered me.

"Did you find what you were looking for?" Annabelle asked as I pulled out my own phone and snapped pictures of her hair.

I shook my head. "No."

Her face fell as she furrowed her brow.

"But don't worry. Let's get you ready, okay?"

We discussed exactly what she wanted done, and I got to work. It felt good to have something else to concentrate on besides a murder as I worked gel into her hair, then gently blow dried it to crimp it. We strategically placed the braids, and I wove in the colorful ribbons. Meanwhile, Annabelle lined her eyes with black and blue eyeliner and applied mascara.

"It looks so good!" she squealed as I emptied half a can of hairspray on her hair.

"It does," I said. "It's like a mixture of Madonna and Boy George. It suits you."

"What do I need to do to convince you to style my hair every day?"

I snorted and shook my head. "You do just fine by yourself. You don't need me."

Having become so engrossed in Annabelle's hair, I hadn't noticed Katrina in the station next to me helping a young girl with her tresses. Our gazes met and she said, "I'm allowing you to stay because I see you're helping your friend. Please don't bring up that unfortunate event while you're here."

"Thank you," I said, smiling. She didn't need to know I was also searching for the killer. "I most certainly won't mention the terrible incident. I'm so happy to be here."

I expected lightning to strike me or my nose to grow substantially. Pants on fire, indeed.

Katrina grunted and returned to brushing the dancer's hair.

"I'm going to use the restroom, Annabelle," I said, laying my hand on her shoulder. "I'll be right back."

"Sounds good," she replied, turning her head in the mirror. "Can you help me with the girls' hair as well? I love what you did here and I'd like to get us all matching hair styles if possible."

"Of course," I said.

While heading to the restroom, I reflected on how odd it felt to have spent so many years in the makeup chair, only to now be on the other side. For a brief moment, a part of me missed the glamour and glitz of my former life. Every day I'd been able to play dress-up and become someone else—a murderer with a somewhat good heart.

"Sam!"

I turned to find Gina making her way through

the crowd. Did she just push that woman out of her way?

"Hey," I greeted once she reached me. "I can't believe all the people here."

She glanced around and shrugged. "It's Heywood. We only have a handful of big events a year that don't revolve around tourists. The Christmas Festival and the Dance Contest being two of them."

"How are things going?" I asked. "How's your new rescue?"

"A pain in my butt," she said. "But I do like him."

"What's his make and model?"

She shook her head. "I have no idea. Maybe some hound or something. Where are you headed?"

"Little girl's room," I said. "Care to join me?"

"Thanks for the intriguing offer, but I'll wait here."

I entered the restroom to find two stalls, one being occupied. I quickly hurried into the second. When the toilet next door flushed, I glanced out the crack between the stall and door to find Starlight. She stood at the mirror dressed in black tights and a matching bodysuit with a pink ballet skirt swirling around her thighs. She ran a hand over her hair, gathered the locks in one hand, then clasped it with a silver star-shaped barrette.

My heart thundered as I stared, it all coming back to me now. The barrette had been in her purse when she knocked it over and it spilled out on the floor before waltzing class had started. I'd actually picked it up and handed it to her.

Trying to be as quiet as possible, I pulled out Jordan's burner phone from my bag hanging on the door and scrolled through the pictures. The barrette matched the one in the crime scene.

I lifted my gaze back to Starlight. Holy smokes. Had I found the murderer?

Starlight smiled at herself in the mirror, then left. Another woman came in shortly after while I sat on the toilet trying to calm my racing heart and gather my wits about me.

After what seemed like ages, I stood and flushed. My body felt creaky, as if I'd been shocked and now found it difficult to put one foot in front of the other. I opened the door and stood where Starlight had been, staring at myself in the mirror. When I finally had the restroom to myself, I placed my palms on the counter, shut my eyes, and took a few deep breaths.

I needed a moment to think things through.

"What the heck, Sam?" Gina said. "Are you sick?"

I shook my head. "No." Realizing this was the perfect opportunity to talk through my reasoning without anyone overhearing me, I said, "Lock the door."

Without questioning me, Gina did as I asked. She met my gaze in the mirror, pushed her tortoiseshell glasses up her nose, and furrowed her brow. "What's going on? I thought you fell in or something. You need a haircut, by the way."

"Listen to me," I said, grabbing her shoulders while ignoring her comment about my curls. "I think I may have just figured out who murdered Brittney."

"How did you do that?" she asked. "You're in a bathroom."

"I know. Starlight came in here and she had a silver star-shaped barrette."

"So?"

"So, there's a deputy at the sheriff's office who texted pictures of the crime scene to Jordan, who then gave me the phone. It matches a barrette found at the crime scene."

Her eyes widened. "Wow, a lot's happened since I last talked to you. I had no idea about the phone. Who is it?"

"I don't know, and it's not important," I said. "Please focus, Gina. The barrette Starlight has in her hair right now is the same barrette that was found at a crime scene!"

"Then how did it get in her hair?" Gina asked. "I mean, wouldn't the police take it if it was at the crime scene? Wouldn't it be in evidence?"

Okay, she had a valid point there. My excitement slowly ebbed, but none of it made sense. "Why does she have a barrette that was found at the crime scene?"

Gina shrugged. "Maybe they're for sale somewhere around town and have become a fashion statement that neither of us are aware of, which wouldn't be a surprise. I mean, look at us." She rolled her eyes and snorted. "Especially you, Miss-I-don't-do-manicures-or-haircuts. For all we know, half the people out in the studio are wearing them."

I glared at her and dismissed her comment. So, my hair was a little wild. It felt good to not worry about my looks, especially since it had been the focus of my life for so many years. "We can't dismiss this," I said. "I feel like we're on to something."

"Well, there's no way to know if the sheriff's

office took the barrette into evidence. You're out of luck there."

But wait. I wasn't out of luck. I rummaged through my bag and pulled out the burner phone. "We'll see about that."

I wish I knew who was on the other end of the dang thing.

DID the police take a silver star-shaped barrette into evidence?

I HAD no idea how long it would take him to answer my text, so I turned the sound up to full and shoved it back into my purse. "Annabelle's waiting for me," I muttered. "I need to help her and the kids get ready."

"The kids?"

"Her backup dancers," I said. "Do you want to come help?"

Gina shrugged and nodded. "Sure. This could be interesting."

I unlocked the bathroom door to find a line of women and girls waiting. "Sorry," I apologized, then hitched a thumb over my shoulder at Gina. "She wasn't feeling well."

"Do you think it stinks in there, Mommy?" a little girl asked loudly. I snickered along with everyone else who was staring at Gina, all probably mulling the answer to the question.

"Nice one, Sam," she said. "Revenge will be swift, though. I can promise you that."

Which reminded me, I needed to tell her about Annabelle's epic revenge on Doctor Butte, but then again, I didn't want to give her any ideas.

"Oh, my gosh, Sam!" Annabelle said when we returned to her table. She'd lined up the girls behind the chair while she worked on another's hair. "I was wondering what happened to you!"

"Sorry, I said, dropping my purse. "There was an… issue."

"What was that?" she asked. I met her gaze and shook my head slightly. Katrina stared at me from over Annabelle's shoulder.

"Nothing," I said. "I'll tell you later." Turning to the next girl in Annabelle's line, I smiled. "Are you ready to get your hair done?"

She nodded and stood next to the chair. Annabelle and I briefly consulted on what I should do with the long blonde locks the girl wore, and then I got to work.

Gina stood next to me, watching me carefully. "I never had to learn to do that since I only had a son. Since you didn't have any kids, where and why did you learn to braid like that?"

I wasn't about to share that I'd spent decades in a makeup chair and having my hair done. Of course, I'd picked up a few tips and tricks during that time. "It comes naturally," I said.

Starlight pushed in through the crowd to Katrina's table. They spoke for a few moments, but I couldn't hear what they said. Starlight turned around to leave, then Katrina yelled, "Starlight! Come back here!"

When the dancer returned, Katrina said, "Where did you get that barrette?"

# CHAPTER 21

WELL, that caught my attention.

Lowering my gaze, I eavesdropped on the conversation and hoped my eyes weren't bugging out of my head. Annabelle stood between me and the two dancers, so I leaned over. "Trade places with me, but don't say anything," I whispered.

She side-eyed me but did as I asked. It only put me about a foot closer to them, but I could hear much better over the din of conversation. Gina stared at me as if I'd lost my mind, but at least she kept her mouth shut. I didn't want to draw attention to the dancers' discussion.

"I found it on the floor," Starlight said. "I put it in lost and found for a while, but it wasn't claimed, so I grabbed it." She reached up and un-clasped her hair. "Is it yours?"

I glanced up and met Katrina's gaze. She stared at me a moment, then returned her attention to Starlight. "No. Go ahead and keep it. Will you help me with this hair, though?"

"Sure," Starlight said, reclasping her hair and stepping up next to her boss. "I love the braids you did on this side."

"Can you do the other, please? I'll be right back."

As Katrina strode—or floated, in her case—away, I glanced over at the girl Starlight now worked on. They chatted a bit while Starlight's fingers moved quickly through the strands.

Had Katrina been lying? Was the barrette really hers? Or maybe it was Gretchen's? And where exactly had Starlight found it? Was it the same one I'd seen in the picture, or was Gina right and it was the new fad in town?

I finished up my dancer's hair and brought another one forward, all the while keeping an eye on Starlight's hands. My chest tightened in desperation. I was missing something and I had a feeling it was right in front of me.

Starlight finished her braid and the dancer stood.

"Can I take a picture of your hair?" I asked.

The girl nodded.

"Let me grab my phone." I hurried over to my bag and pulled it out, then snapped a few pictures of the braided updo. "You look great. Good luck in the contest."

"You're supposed to say, break a leg," the girl countered.

I'd always hated that expression, so it never left my lips. I understood the history, but it seemed so wrong to tell someone good luck by busting limbs. "Well, I really don't hope you crack your tibia, but I'm looking forward to watching you dance."

An hour later, Annabelle's crew had their hair done and Gina and I found two seats in the audience.

"You're acting really weird," Gina said.

"I feel like the clues to who killed Brittney are right here in front of me and I can't figure them out." I sighed and crossed my arms over my chest. "I'm so frustrated right now, I just want to kick someone."

"Stay the heck away from my shins, please."

Katrina took the stage holding a microphone and a piece of paper, smiling ear-to-ear. "Welcome to Groove and Go Dance! My name's Katrina and I'm the owner. I'd like to thank you all for coming out and supporting our dancers. I think we're going to have an amazing show for you. Without further ado, let's begin." She glanced at her paper. "First off, we have the Little Toe Tappers, who have come to us from Sedona to participate. Please give them a warm welcome!"

As the girls, ranging from probably about six to ten, pranced out on the stage, the crowd erupted in applause. Dressed in striped black and white bodysuits, they reminded me of skinny zebras.

"It looks like they all just escaped from prison," Gina whispered. "A very unfortunate costume choice."

Zebras, prisoners... either way she was right. A poor costume choice, indeed.

The Little Toe Tappers lived up to their name, tapdancing across the stage into the hearts of the judges, who scored them with nines and tens.

"So impressive!" Katrina said before introducing the next dancers. "We have our own Molly and Vernon Fitzsimmons here today to show you how waltzing is done right!"

"They were in our waltzing class," I said, recognizing the elderly couple and elbowing Gina. "Remember them?"

She shook her head. "I was concentrating on keep my toes intact, clodhopper. I didn't have time to look at anyone else."

I rolled my eyes and tried to focus on the dancing, but waltzing wasn't my thing and I quickly lost interest. Glancing around the audience, I was happy to see the number of people who'd come out to support the local dancers, and those who had traveled from outside areas. Heywood really came together for their events, and it gave me pride to be a member of the community. Unlike Hollywood folks, who ate their own. Hello, bitterness, my old friend.

When applause broke out, I turned my attention back to the stage to find Katrina introducing the next act. A group of Heywood's ballet dancers ranging from toddler age to about ten ascended the stage and took their places, each dressed in pink from head to toe and looking like quite the ballet troupe. The ones with long hair had it done up in intricate braids, and all had pink circles on each of their cheeks. The girls reminded me of a doll collection one of my childhood friends had.

As the music began, everyone moved in sync. A moment later, the smallest girl, about three or four, decided she was going to do her own thing. She broke ranks and did her own dance which included a lot of jerking and wiggling, very contrarian to the girls behind her moving fluidly.

The audience burst out laughing, which only fueled her on. On the side of the stage, Katrina hissed at her, but I couldn't hear what she was saying. Based on the color of her cheeks, she wasn't happy.

"That little girl is my spirit animal," Gina said, laughing.

I smiled, but my concentration was on Katrina. A grin was plastered on her face, but her body language said she wanted to kill the kid messing up her recital.

For the first time, I saw a side of her I'd never seen. Veins popped in her neck while her whole body tensed and muscles rippled under her skin as she motioned the little contrarian to the side of the stage.

Finally, the music stopped and an audience member I assumed to be her father jumped up on the stage and grabbed the little girl. He marched her into the back room while she screamed at the top of her lungs.

"Poor thing," Gina said, still giggling. "She had her spotlight taken away."

The room still tittered with laughter as Katrina took a few deep breaths and hurried up to the stage to organize her dancers once again. Once the music began, she returned to her place on the side.

I quickly learned ballet without a trouble-causing toddler wasn't my thing either, and I lost interest while my thoughts returned to the barrette.

Before I went accusing anyone of murder, I needed to know if the hair clasp at the murder scene had been picked up by the sheriff's office. I had to assume it had been and it was just a fluke that the same barrette was now on Starlight's head.

I picked up my bag from the floor and dug around for the burner phone. Keeping it inside the purse so no one else could catch a glimpse of it, I checked for messages from my mysterious deputy. To my surprise, I had a notification from him. I hadn't heard the phone buzz or anything, but then again, I'd been watching a three-year-old blow up a dance recital, which so far was the most exciting thing to happen.

No barrette listed *on the evidence report.*

. . .

My BREATH CAUGHT in my throat. Jordan had said he was first on the scene and Mallory had taken him off the case because of Brittney's sexual assault allegations against him.

If the police hadn't gathered the barrette as evidence, then did that mean Starlight was walking around with the one I'd noticed in the pictures? She'd said she'd found it. I had to know where.

"I'll be right back," I whispered to Gina as a group of teens took to the stage.

Hip Hop blasted through the speakers while I grabbed my bag and made my way through the crowd in search of Starlight. Time for me to start asking some hard questions.

I found her in the back room and smiled as I approached. Crossing her arms over her chest, she stared at me with her lips in a thin line.

"What do you want?" she asked in a curt tone.

My original plan had been to play nice and engage in a little small talk, but her attitude bristled the hairs on the back of my neck. I could be rude, too. "Where did you get that barrette?"

"Why?" she asked.

"Just curious. My friend has one just like it, and it's missing." Liar, liar, pants on fire. But I could also see I was rattling her.

She narrowed her gaze. "Are you suggesting I stole it?"

"Did you?"

"No," she said, straightening her shoulders. "How dare you imply such a thing?"

"I had to ask. I mean, it looks just like the one found at the murder scene."

Her eyes widened as she gasped. Many emotions ran over her face at breakneck speed. Surprise, worry, indignity... and she ended up on worried. "What... what do you mean?"

Leaning in so my mouth almost touched her ear, I whispered, "I know that barrette was at the murder scene. I have the proof. All I need to do is figure out who it belonged to, and then I'll have caught the true killer."

"It's not mine!" She tore it out of her hair and threw it to the floor. "I found it!"

"We'll see about that." I turned on my heel and headed for Katrina's office. Before pushing open the door, I glanced over my shoulder to see her walking in, headed directly for Starlight. She apparently hadn't seen me.

Shutting the door behind me, I hurried over to her desk and quickly rummaged through all the drawers, where I found a silver star-shaped barrette.

I stared at it a moment, debating whether to leave it or take it. Leave. Evidence shouldn't be messed with. It was a good find and solidified the barrette Starlight wore most likely belonged to Katrina, but I still couldn't prove who the killer was. I felt certain I could rule out Starlight, but that didn't mean I couldn't exclude her boyfriend, Rocky. Nor could I dismiss Katrina or Gretchen as the killers. Both knew how to braid quite well.

Besides, this barrette could've been found and Katrina was keeping it until someone claimed it.

But I didn't think so.

Wait a minute.

Braids.

Dang it. Sometimes I just wanted to slap myself across the face. With a curse, I pulled out my phone and the burner, then pulled up the pictures of the murder weapon, as well as the girls' hairstyle Starlight and Katrina had worked on.

And with great certainty, I knew I'd found the murderer. But how would I get a confession?

I typed to my mystery deputy.

*I THINK I know who the killer is. I'm at the dance studio right now. I think it's—*

· · ·

THE DOOR swung open and Katrina's hard gaze met mine. *Uh oh.* I was in trouble. Instead of hitting send, I dialed the number and set the phone down on the desk as I stepped forward, hoping to hide the device behind me.

"Hey!" I said, smiling at her. "What's up? I hope you don't mind me using your office, Katrina. I just needed a minute to myself."

"I asked you not to speak to anyone about Brittney's demise."

"And I haven't," I said innocently.

"Why are you questioning Starlight about the barrette?"

I shrugged and stepped toward her. "Like I said, my friend has one that's similar and she lost it."

"You also told her it was the same one found at the murder scene."

"Yes, that's what I heard. It's too bad our sheriff is such an imbecile, she didn't find it, right? I bet there was a bunch of DNA on there that could've led to the killer." I clucked my tongue and shook my head. "But guess what else is interesting?"

She didn't answer.

"The ribbons that were used to kill Brittney," I said. "I know who made them."

Katrina snorted and rolled her eyes. "Oh, you do? This should be good."

"You did," I replied. "See, I compared the ribbon in the crime scene photo to the braids you did on the girl this morning. And do you want to know what I discovered?"

A flicker of fear came and went in her eyes.

"You're left-handed," I said, not bothering to wait for her to answer me. "And so was the killer."

# CHAPTER 22

KATRINA STARED at me a long moment, her face turning the same color as it had when the three-year-old had taken over her ballet recital.

I continued, "And I also found a matching barrette in your top desk drawer… yep. The same one that should've been picked up at the murder scene."

I'd laid out all my evidence, which wasn't much, but I knew deep in my soul Katrina had murdered Brittney because she'd stolen from her. What I hadn't anticipated was her lunging at me, then wrapping her hands around my throat.

I yelped as I fell backwards on top of the desk while Katrina straddled me as if she were my second skin. While I tried to pull her hands off my windpipe, she growled, "You won't be around to share your theories."

Well, her attack pretty much solidified her guilt in my book.

The strength possessed by the woman scared me to death. While filming As The Years Turn, there'd been many scenes where people had tried to choke my character, but it had all been acting. I wasn't sure what to do when being caught in the real-life situation.

Recalling my self-defense course, I released her wrist, then shoved the palm of my hand upward toward her nose… and missed. Then, I slapped the side of her face with one hand while fighting her grip around my throat with the other. Wrapping my legs around her, I slammed my heel into her back. Nothing seemed to lessen her rage. The woman was an evil force of nature and stronger than I could've imagined.

I realized this was the same anger that had fueled her during Brittney's killing. The victim must have fought long and hard but despite their age difference, Katrina had overpowered her.

I wouldn't allow that to happen to me. She wouldn't take my do-over in life away from me. Heywood had given me too much to live for.

Feeling around the desk, I picked up the

keyboard and smashed it against the side of her head. It knocked her off balance for a second, long enough for her grip to lessen and me to catch my breath. But then, she was right back on me. I swung the keyboard at her again, but she grabbed it and tossed it across the room.

I then found something round and hard on the desk and jammed it right into her forehead. It sent her toppling off me and onto the floor. As I fought to sit up, I glanced at the object. A ballerina in a snow globe small enough to fit into the palm of my hand had saved me. I struggled to catch my breath while Katrina lay moaning on the floor.

The police. I had to call the police.

Where had my phone gone?

I glanced around and found the burner on the floor. I fell to my knees and crawled over to it, surprised to hear jazz music playing from the speaker. I slowly picked it up and brought it to my ear.

"Hello?" I whispered.

At that moment, the office door flung open and a man wearing jeans and a t-shirt burst in, a gun in one hand and a phone in the other. Dropping the burner, I held my hands up to my shoulders as his hard gaze swept the room. "Sam, are there any weapons in the room?"

I shook my head as it slowly dawned on me that this may be my mysterious deputy and there was jazz music playing in the main studio for the dance competition. "She tried to kill me," I said, my voice ragged.

"I know. I heard it all. Good idea leaving the phone on."

As he squatted next to Katrina, Gina ran in. "Sam! Are you okay?"

I nodded, feeling as though I'd entered some surreal moment where I'd barely escaped death. "How did you know where I was?"

She hitched a thumb over her shoulder. "Trevor here got me out of the audience."

"Jordan said if you weren't with Annabelle, I'd find you with Gina," the man said. "When I came into the studio, I didn't see Annabelle but I spotted Gina right away. She and I go way back."

I lowered myself so I lay on the floor, staring up at the ceiling.

"When you left me, I took note of which way you went," Gina said. "Then Trevor grabbed me and I brought him back here. He heard the commotion through the door and we swept in to save you."

"She didn't need saving," Trevor said, winking at me as he hauled a sobbing Katrina to her feet. "Sam had everything under control."

Had I? Not even close. However, I didn't have the energy to argue. If he wanted to believe I was some type of super-ninja woman, then so be it.

"I'm taking Katrina down to the station to book her," Trevor said. "I'd sure hate to ruin the dance contest by parading her out the front. Is there a back door?"

"Yes. Yes, there is," I rasped, sitting up and struggling to stand. I'd forgotten about the dance contest. "Please, use it. For Annabelle's sake, the dance contest has to go on without interruption."

"How are we going to do that with the hostess going to jail?" Gina asked.

Goodness, my throat ached. "Tell Starlight Katrina isn't feeling well and have her do the introductions. We have to keep it going for Annabelle." My voice sounded like sandpaper.

Gina sprang into action while I led Trevor to the back door.

"I haven't thanked you yet for saving my life," I said. If looks could kill, I'd be dead on the floor from Katrina's stare.

"Glad I could be of assistance," Trevor replied.

"Again, smart to use the burner to call me and leave it on."

"Thanks." My cheeks warmed at the compliment.

"You know, Jordan talks about you non-stop. Says you're one of the smartest people he's ever met, and it looks like he's right. Nice job solving this murder and clearing his name."

I nodded, certain my face resembled a tomato.

As I showed him where the back door was, I gently touched my throat. I'd be bruised for sure, but had there been internal damage? I didn't have a doctor to check me out, and the last person I wanted touching me was Doctor Butte, especially if he suspected Annabelle and me being behind the dead fish incident in his car.

After waving Trevor off, I hurried back into the main studio where I heard Starlight introduce the Totally Awesome Annabelle and her Cool Crew. I snickered at the name she'd given herself and took a seat just as Michael Jackson's "Beat It" began playing.

Complete with a hat, silver glove, ankle-high leather pants and matching jacket, Annabelle glided across the stage while keeping her head down. Her backup dancers, all dressed in black, mimicked her every move. After about a minute,

Annabelle ripped off her hat and leather jacket, tossed them aside, and became Madonna.

The crowd rose to its feet as she gyrated and posed, giving us all a come-hither stare while a montage of Madonna songs played. Once again, her backup dancers were right there with her. Despite almost dying just moments ago, I found myself clapping and moving along with the rest of the audience. She ended with a haunting dance to "When Doves Cry" by Prince and received a standing ovation at the end.

Tears welled in my eyes as Annabelle took her bow, but I couldn't figure out why I was crying.

Then it hit me.

Pride.

I was so proud of my friend.

When in Hollywood, I knew when I won an award, those clapping for me were doing so for the television cameras. None of my friends had ever been proud of me, or me of them. Disappointed? Yes. Envious? Definitely. But celebrating someone's accomplishments with sheer joy hadn't been a part of my life there.

Once again, I appreciated the authenticity of Heywood and my real emotions toward the friends I'd made.

After Annabelle brought down the house, another dance troupe had to follow. Nowhere near as good, they received polite applause and I felt bad for them. It would be hard to follow Totally Awesome Annabelle and her Cool Crew.

As Annabelle accepted her trophy—a gold one standing about a foot high with a ballet dancer on top—I wondered when Jordan would be cut loose and what Mallory would say about her epic mistake. Would he get an apology? I doubted it.

Someone had to run against her, though. There was no way she'd resign. Had there been other people who'd been sent away for crimes they didn't commit under her watch? Most likely. It seemed she couldn't catch a killer if her life depended on it.

After accepting her award, Annabelle came off the stage to greet Gina and me. She squealed in delight as she held up her trophy and I gave her a big hug, as did Gina.

"You guys were great, Annabelle!" I said.

Her smile fading, she narrowed her gaze. "What happened to your neck?"

Gina and I traded glances, and I shook my head. "I'll tell you about it later. For now, let's go celebrate you being this year's best dancer in Heywood."

# EPILOGUE

SUMMER PASSED in the blink of an eye. The deck was completed, and I loved every blessed second I was able to spend out there either by myself or with my friends watching the river go by, or waiting on our customers. It hadn't been as profitable as I'd hoped, but I didn't regret the money I'd sunk into it.

Before I knew it, I was smack-dab in the middle of the Christmas holiday and gearing up for the Annual Christmas Festival.

As Annabelle and I headed over to the Heywood Community Center to set out our handmade gift baskets with the hope people would buy them, I worried what Christmas gifts to buy for Annabelle and Gina, as well as Deputy Jordan Branson, who may have been my boyfriend—if I dated. I spent enough time with him for him to earn that title.

Once we arrived at the Community Center, I exited the car and glanced upward as snow began to fall once again, the flakes hitting my cheeks.

"I wonder where everyone is?" Annabelle asked, opening the trunk to her car. "I thought more store owners would be here to set up their tables."

Glancing around the parking lot, I realized we were the only ones there. "Maybe they'll stop by later."

I grabbed as many baskets as I could carry and carefully treaded through the calf-high snow. Unfortunately, the town snowplow had some mechanical issues and hadn't been able to clear the roads and parking lots in two days. While the gentle flakes continued their beautiful descent, cold silence engulfed us. A chill ran down my spine and I felt as if we were the only two people left in Heywood... or in the middle of a horror movie.

Lights blazed from the Community Center ahead and when we got closer, I heard "Silent

Night" playing from within. Hopefully, set up would be quick and easy as I was longing to curl up on my couch with Catnip and have a glass of wine or two. My shoulders slumped with exhaustion, and I realized the holidays were a lot of work. In my former Hollywood life, I'd simply passed the duties to my housekeeper.

Annabelle balanced her baskets on her leg and pulled open the door. Once inside, we stamped our boots on the large red welcome rug to remove the snow.

"The wood floor gets a little slick when it's wet, so watch your step," Annabelle warned.

Great. Just what I needed—another fall. I'd already had three since the snow started about two months ago, and my distaste for winter grew with each day. I loved looking at the snow—I just didn't like trying to live my life in it.

We walked through the foyer, hung a right, and headed for the big gymnasium. A strange odor of pine needles, cinnamon, and sweaty shoes engulfed us the closer we got, causing me to grimace. It was my understanding that the boys' basketball teams often practiced here, which explained the sweaty shoe smell.

When we entered the gym, I gasped, forgetting the odor. Never would I have imagined a gym could look so pretty.

A large Christmas tree standing at least twenty feet tall twinkled in the middle of the basketball court while thousands of tiny lights had been strung across the ceiling and along the walls, all glittering and giving off enough illumination so the harsh, fluorescent lights weren't necessary. In a corner sat two high back red velvet chairs with golden and silver intricacies woven in, placed on a red and green rug. "That's for Santa and his wife," Annabelle said, pointing at them. "Last year they had elves as well. I don't know if they'll do that this time, though."

"Why is that?"

"Well, Santa, like, has a bit of a drinking problem and he and one of the elves he'd been boozing with got into a fistfight."

"Oh, my." I didn't know whether to laugh or be appalled.

"Yes. They were rolling on the floor with fists swinging, cursing at each other. It wasn't one of Heywood's finest moments."

"Why don't they find a new Santa?" I asked.

"Wait until you see him," she said. "You couldn't find a more perfect Santa. He's been playing the role for fifteen years now and loves it. He plans for it all year."

Along the walls sat empty tables. I noted a few had been decorated with tablecloths and had goods arranged on them. "Looks like we aren't the first ones here."

"Apparently not," Annabelle, replied. "Let's find our table. Hopefully we've got a good one close to the door."

We found our spot along with two, fold out metal chairs labeled Sage Advice, fourth in from the door, in between Jemisphere, the local jewelry shop, and Locked and Loaded, the gun store.

"This is great!" Annabelle said as we set down our baskets and purses, then stripped out of our coats.

"Who's going to buy someone a gun for Christmas?" I asked, pointing at the Locked and Loaded table.

"Your California mentality is showing," Annabelle muttered, rolling her eyes. "I love getting guns and gear to go with them for Christmas."

Huh. Well, at least I knew what to put under the tree for her.

As Annabelle danced around to "Rockin' Around the Christmas Tree" coming through the gymnasium speakers, we set out our own table-cloth—green with red and silver trim bearing the store's name—to cover the old, worn table.

Our gift baskets were tied with red or green bows, a sneaky idea we'd come up with while preparing them. A red bow meant one price, a green bow meant another. That way we'd know on sight how much to charge the customer. Genius, if you asked me.

We arranged the display, adding a few embellishments like the dish full of candy canes and some bows we pinned on the front of the table-cloth surrounding the store's name, as well as a string of small white lights to border the front. We then placed our inventory underneath and stepped back to admire our work.

"That looks fantastic," Annabelle said. Glancing around at the other tables, she leaned in and whispered, "Much better than the other ones that have been set up."

I nodded in agreement. "Let's go take a closer look."

We walked around, stopping at Knit Wit's table to check out her offerings. Since the physical store sat next to mine out on Comfort Road, I knew the owner, Mrs. Mason, well. She was offering knitted dolls and discounts on knitting classes.

"Gina's going to try to adopt out some of her rescues," I said, pointing at a sign that read Heywood Hounds, the name of Gina's rescue business.

The next table took us to the other side of the gym where we found Too Hot to Handle, a hot sauce joint.

"I wonder how hot that Devil's Juice is," Annabelle said, pointing to the jar. "I imagine it would fry off your eyebrows."

"Probably." I turned to glance at the tree and a scream stuck in my throat as I grabbed Annabelle's arm.

"What?" she asked.

I pointed at the tree, all words stuck in my throat. Dread and horror slumped my shoulders and caused my stomach to lurch.

"Oh no!" she yelled. We ran over to find a woman dressed in a Santa suit staring up at the ceiling with milky, dead eyes, a small pool of blood surrounding her head. Annabelle fell to her knees and felt for a pulse, but I already knew the answer.

She turned and looked up at me, tears brimming in her eyes. "Why? Who in the world would kill Mrs. Claus?"

WHO, indeed?

Find out who killed Mrs. Claus and what happens at the Heywood Christmas Festival in Mistletoe and Mayhem, available at your favorite retailers.

# ALSO BY CARLY WINTER

The Heywood Herbalist Cozy Mysteries

(Small town contemporary cozies)

From Hollywood, California, to Heywood, Arizona, trouble follows her…

After her husband's brutal killing and her fall from the Hollywood elite, the disgraced Samantha Rathbone moves to Heywood, Arizona, hoping to forget her past and live a quiet life of anonymity.

It doesn't go as planned.

Sedona Spirt Mysteries

(Paranormal cozies)

Bernie and the ghost of her dead grandmother find themselves in the middle of various murder investigations. Danger and hilarity ensues as the crazy duo follow the clues to discover the killers.

The Tri-Town Murders

(Small town contemporary cozies)

Complete Series

Follow newspaper reporter Tilly and her group of fun,

quirky friends as they solve murders in a fictional, small town in California.

Killer Skies Mysteries

Set in 1965, join Patty Briggs, stewardess extraordinaire, as she flies the skies and solves murders with the help of her friends… and one cute FBI agent!

# ABOUT THE AUTHOR

USA Today bestselling author Carly Winter writes fun, small town cozy mysteries, always with a dash of humor and quirky characters. When not writing, you can find her spending time with her family, on a Pilates reformer or enjoying the fantastic Arizona weather (except summer - she doesn't like summer). She does like dogs, wine and chocolate and wishes Christmas happened twice a year.

To be notified of new releases, book recommendations, to learn more about Carly and for your chance to win giveaways, join her exclusive cozy mystery author report.

For more information on her books, please visit: CarlyWinterCozyMysteries.com

www.ingramcontent.com/pod-product-compliance
Lightning Source LLC
Chambersburg PA
CBHW011034190726
48290CB00011B/2848